Presumption of Guilt

There were formless mists as he became aware of himself. Then there was pain, at first remote, but all too soon immediate. Someone murmured meaningless but comforting words: the mists closed in and there was nothing.

Later there was form. A room with a high ceiling and a central light with a frilly, plastic shade which made him think of Brighton boarding-houses. He stared at the shade and tried to work out how he could have come to be faced by such a monstrosity, but the pounding pain in his head had made the problem too difficult. He closed his eyes and drifted off into an uneasy sleep that was filled with violent nightmares.

JEFFREY ASHFORD

Presumption of Guilt

WALKER AND COMPANY · NEW YORK

All the characters and events portrayed in this story are fictitious.

First published in the United States of America in 1985 by the Walker Publishing Company, Inc.

This paperback edition first published in 1986.

ISBN: 0-8027-3150-3

Library of Congress Catalog Card Number: 84-25747

Printed in the United States of America

10 9 8 7 6 5 4 3 2 1

CHAPTER 1

Eight years previously, Cala Survas had been described in an illustrated Sunday supplement as the last undiscovered bay on the Costa Brava. The article had not explained how a bay could be both undiscovered and described in such detail, but the succeeding eight years rendered any such explanation superfluous. All the benefits of advanced civilization arrived in the form of package-tour hotels and apartment blocks, restaurants and cafés, supermarkets and drink stores, shoe and memento shops, and plastic litter. Cala Survas had definitely been discovered.

The land between the town and the mountains undulated and on many of the more elevated sites luxurious villas had been built. These were occupied by wealthy foreigners who sought the services which fuelled the tourist industry—telephones, central heating, flush lavatories, imported foods, maids who spoke their languages—but who were unwilling to live in close proximity to the tourists. Casa Bellini was one such villa. It lay a kilometre beyond the outskirts of the town and was a strange jumble of roof levels and awkward angles—strangely, this complete lack of symmetry lent a touch of charm, unusual since it had been designed by a Spanish architect.

Angus Sterne, seated on the fireplace side of the card table, picked up the five cards he'd just been dealt. Three kings, an ace, and a five. Three kings never lost.

'Let's be havin' some cards, then,' said Smedley, their host, northern accent broad. 'I'm feeling right lucky.'

'I'll have three, please,' said the middle-aged Pascall. Monet dealt him the cards. He picked them up, looked briefly at them, then added them to his other two and put all five face down on the table.

'And two for me. The little babies I want.' Cánaves, the only Spaniard present, spoke a mixture of English and American. His Zapata moustache added a touch of lawlessness to his swarthy, handsome face. It was his proud boast that he bedded a different tourist—female—every night of the season.

'One,' said Smedley. When he'd looked at it, he chuckled. 'This is going to cost you.'

'Three,' said Evans.

Sterne wondered—did he buy two cards or keep a kicker? If he bought two it would signal the likelihood that he had three of a kind; if he bought one it would probably be assumed that he had two pairs or was trying to fill a straight or a flush. 'One, please.' He discarded the five and kept the ace. He was dealt another five. Life, he decided, had a warped sense of humour.

'The dealer, he take two cards,' said Monet. He was a small, precise man, very formal in manner.

'Well?' said Smedley loudly.

'Pass,' said Pascall.

'Five 'undred,' said Cánaves, as always failing to pronounce the 'h'.

'Chicken-feed,' sneered Smedley.

'Or sucker-bait?' suggested Evans.

Smedley pushed forward five large chips. 'Five thousand,' he said challengingly.

'You're forgetting the limit's a thousand a rise,' said Evans.

'We decided there'd be no limit on the last round.'

'Did we?'

'What's the trouble? Getting too hot for a penny-ante player?'

Evans increased his stake to two large chips and three one-thousand-peseta notes. 'I'm seeing.'

Smedley, Sterne thought, had been losing steadily and he was a man who couldn't bear ever to lose. So now he was trying to pile-drive his way back to profit. In front of Sterne were twenty thousand pesetas in notes and chips—he'd been winning quietly but steadily. Apart from his 'emergency fund' that was all the money he had. But three kinds never lost. 'Make it six thousand.'

Monet threw in.

'Chicken!' said Smedley loudly. He wasn't drunk, but neither was he sober. He'd refilled his own glass more often than his guests' and during the evening his manner had become belligerent as well as loud.

'I'm away,' said Pascall, as he threw in his cards.

Smedley's tone became more scornful. 'We start playing real poker and everyone quits.' He turned to Cánaves. 'Are you running for cover?'

'Me? I have not the cards for such stakes.'

'You mean, you fold when the pressure starts to hurt.'

Cánaves brushed his moustache with his right forefinger. He had a fierce pride and did not willingly suffer an insult unanswered but, typically Spanish, he would remain silent rather than be rude to his host.

Smedley fanned out his cards and studied them, then pushed all his chips forward.

'How much is there?' asked Evans.

'Hang on, lad. I've not finished yet. When I get a good hand I want everyone to know about it.' He chuckled as he reached into the right-hand pocket of his linen trousers and brought out a roll of notes. He counted. 'Make it seventy-five thousand.' Despite the air-conditioning, on maximum setting, beads of sweat began to form on his forehead.

Evans said: 'That's not on, Hugh.'

'What d'you mean?'

'This is a friendly game. A bet like that stops it being friendly.'

'Jesus! This is poker, not beggar-my-neighbour.'

'I'll see six thousand.'

'I've put it up to seventy-five thousand. Meet that or quit.'

Evans threw in his cards.

Smedley turned to Sterne. 'Are you chicken?' It was as much a triumphant statement of fact as a question and he reached out to sweep up the money.

'I've not bet yet.'

There was a sudden sense of tension as they realized that Smedley might not be allowed to bully his way to winning after all.

'D'you think you'll make your mind up by bloody tomorrow?' Smedley came to his feet, clumsily pushed back the chair, went over to the mobile cocktail cabinet and refilled his glass with a brandy and soda. The sweat began to roll down his fleshy face as he sat once more.

Smedley had taken one card, Sterne thought, so he'd had two pairs, three of a kind and had kept a kicker (his style of play suggested he seldom went in for the subtlety of a kicker), four to a straight, flush, or straight flush, or four of a kind. The odds against four of a kind were very high, whether he'd held them originally or the single card had matched the threes he'd had before: buying one to a straight flush happened only in daydreams: so that left two pairs, three of a kind and a kicker, or four to a straight or flush: the last card might have turned two pairs into a full house, but the odds were all against: three of a kind might be aces, but his own discard had been an ace which made it unlikely: the kicker might have been matched for a full house, but that was even more unlikely: buying the fifth card to a flush or straight was always ten times as difficult as the odds said it should be . . . Smedley had either two pairs or three of a kind, lower than kings. Three kings were never beaten.

'Well?' demanded Smedley.

'I'll see you.'

Smedley finished the brandy and put his glass down heavily on the small table by his side. 'Where's the colour of your money, then?'

'There's twenty thousand here and the rest is at my flat.'

'I'm not bloody well playing for tick.'

'Are you saying Angus hasn't got the money at his flat?' asked Evans contemptuously.

Smedley backed away from so direct a challenge. 'No. I'm just sayin' . . .'

'Then turn your cards over.'

Smedley began to sweat even more freely at the unwelcome thought that he might after all be going to lose. Reluctantly, he showed a low straight.

'Good enough,' Sterne said.

CHAPTER 2

Sterne woke and stared at the closed shutters of the studio room, picked out by the harsh sunshine beyond. After a while, his thoughts coalesced and he considered the two hundred and fifty pounds he owed Smedley. There wasn't much more than that in his emergency fund. Certainly, he was going to be left with less than the cost of his ticket back to the UK: his ticket back to a regular, respectable life . . .

Had he been tight and was that why he'd seen Smedley's hand, thereby losing seventy-five thousand pesetas? But he could remember clearly all that had happened, even down to the logic of his thoughts as he'd decided Smedley must have had two pairs or losing threes. So it hadn't been drink which had egged him on to financial disaster. Then had it been the desire to wipe the smile off Smedley's face? Bumptious, cocky people like Smedley usually evoked that kind of a reaction. And life, loving a joke, sometimes made certain that the desire turned out to be an expensive one . . . Bugger that miserable six-high straight! At least it might have been a decent one, say jack high, to make its victory seem more impressive and therefore slightly more palatable.

He mentally calculated figures and decided that after he'd settled with Smedley he'd have about eighteen thousand pesetas left. A flight home at this time of the year, by a local charter firm, cost around twenty-two thousand. It was virtually impossible to feed and drink—in this heat, water was about as satisfying as dried acorn coffee—on less than twelve hundred pesetas a day. In five days' time, his next month's rent would be due in advance. His landlady was a delightful old woman, full of good humour and a dry wit, but when it came to money she could have taught Shylock a thing or two . . .

It looked as if he'd have to phone Ralph again and ask for more money. And Ralph would point out, pontifically, that it was only a month now since he'd forwarded a thousand pounds from the trust which had been meant to last at least three months. Three months? Ralph had not met Sonia or he'd never have suggested such an impossibility. Sonia treated money with the contempt it deserved. But then Ralph probably didn't know such people existed. How could he, sitting at his desk, surrounded by wills, deeds, conveyances, contracts, statutes, pleadings, and opinions, and never the time to look out through the window at far horizons? Sterne laughed at the thought of introducing Sonia to Ralph: and at Angela's reactions to the introduction . . .

The first time he'd met Angela he'd correctly summed her up. Middle class and middle course. Not that he'd disliked her—he'd felt sorry for her. And unfortunately she'd realized this. He could still recall the look she'd given him, on that first meeting, when she'd said that she couldn't stay long. No visit to Ralph's bedroom to view the etchings: in an age of permissiveness, she practised chastity. And that look had told him something more. That she knew that if it had been he who had had a girl in for drinks they'd have been studying those etchings as soon as possible, and she despised him, but also envied him, for the gusto with which he drained the cup of life . . .

Left to himself, Ralph would forward another and generous cheque, together with a brief, forgettable sermon. Although outwardly he was a sober, hardworking, conventional solicitor, married to a woman whose creed was loyalty before everything, father of a charming, precocious daughter, owner of an Elizabethan farmhouse, generous contributor to Conservative party funds, reader of *The Times* and *Country Life*, there was buried deep within his being a yearning to experience just a few of the piquancies of life. And if he could not indulge in them directly, then he welcomed the chance of doing so vicariously, through his younger brother . . . But Ralph was never left to himself. Angela was his partner in everything. And she would point out that his brother had wasted more than enough time and money so he must send no more money now than was absolutely necessary to make certain Angus returned straight back home and began to work . . .

Sterne climbed out of bed, crossed to the window, opened the shutters and swung them back on to their catches. The sunlight warmed his face as he looked down the road, past a palm tree, and at the travel-poster-blue sea in the bay. He recognized that life could not always be like this, that the dividing line between the man who was sampling life and the drifter could become too thin, but he wasn't yet ready to submerge himself in the ordered, aseptic world of the trusted, steady wage-earner. He laughed aloud. 'Give me chastity and continency, but do not give it yet.' He wanted to meet more Sonias. How many Sonias dare one meet?

There was a knock on the door and when he called out, Evans entered. Evans said: 'With all the merriment, I thought you must have at least one woman in here.'

'Only in my imagination.'

'You might lend me your imagination some time.' Evans crossed to a rush-bottomed chair and sat. 'I'm sorry you lost that hand last night. I was hoping you'd take that stupid bastard to the cleaners . . . If it's not a rude question, what had you?'

'Three kings.'

'But three kings never lose.'

'You know that and I know that, but someone forgot to tell the cards.'

'Hugh'll be telling everyone he's the finest poker-player this side of Houston.'

'The higher they climb, the further they fall.'

'And I want to be there to give him a push . . . He was talking about another game before we left last night. He'll be so cocky he'll end up flat on his arse. So how about organizing the pleasure?'

'You'll have to count me out.'

'Are you sure?'

'Couldn't be more certain.' Sterne crossed to a second chair and picked up his clothes. 'I'm taking a quick shower. You'll hang on for a drink, won't you?'

'Mention liquor and I become immovable.'

As he showered, Sterne wondered why Evans had called. Surely not just to find out what hand he'd had? Since he'd first met Evans, he'd often tried to place the man and every time had failed. Evans had plenty of money, but never gave the slightest hint where it had come from. He had the easy self-confidence of a man who'd learned to handle any situation, but never made the slightest reference to his past life. To that extent, he was no different from many expatriates to be found around the Mediterranean. But what singled him out was an occasional glimpse of calculating, withdrawn watchfulness: a friendly man who never allowed himself the luxury of a friend.

Refreshed, dressed in T-shirt, jeans, and flip-flops, Sterne returned to the studio room. 'There's brandy, gin, rum, or beer.'

'A brandy and soda, please . . . Are you handing over the rest of the money to Hugh?'

Sterne, now standing by the side of the heavy Spanish sideboard, turned, a bottle of Soberano in his right hand. 'Of course I am.'

'At the start of the game, we agreed a limit of a thousand a rise and a ten thousand maximum. D'you remember him saying anything about forgetting the limit on the last round?'

'Can't say I do.'

'No more do I.'

'It's probably because he serves king-sized drinks.'

Evans shook his head. 'It's because he never said it. He only claimed he did because he needed to win and without a limit he could use his money like a sledgehammer. There's no call for you to pay him a peseta more than ten thousand.'

Sterne turned back, poured out two brandies, added soda and ice, and carried the glasses across. He sat down on the bed.

'You've paid him twenty mil already. Ask for ten back.'

'I'm not going to do that.'

'Why not? Are you rolling in money?'

'Far from it.'

'Then?'

He tried to conceal his growing irritation at the way in which Evans was pursuing the matter. 'As I see things, it doesn't matter what we agreed at the beginning. Hugh called seventy-five thou and I saw him. By seeing him, I was implicitly agreeing to the change of rules, if there was such a change.'

'Shall I tell you what I'd do in your place? I'd tell the stupid bastard to go whistle since he twisted the rules to suit himself . . . You're too honest.'

'It's not like that,' said Sterne, feeling that he was being made to look slightly ridiculous even though he was doing what, by his own lights, was right.

'Let's forget it,' said Evans, as if it had not been he who'd introduced the subject. 'What are you doing for lunch?'

Until Ralph sent him some money, lunch was going to have to consist of bread, cheese, and a bottle of vino corriente. 'Eating on the beach.'

'Have it in a restaurant on me.' Evans stood. 'Let's say one o'clock at Mateo's and over a drink or two we'll decide where to move on to to eat.' He left.

Sterne wondered why the luncheon invitation, from a man who until now had never been more than casually polite. A friendly pick-you-up for someone who'd lost a sizeable sum of money the night before and was obviously now nearly broke? It hardly seemed in character. Evans surely was someone who saw the world as a place in which each man was left to paddle his own canoe, successfully or unsuccessfully. Yet it was difficult to imagine what ulterior motive for the invitation there could be . . .

He crossed to the sideboard and poured himself another brandy. He must work out what to say to Ralph, knowing that Angela would be very ready to express her thoughts on the subject.

Mateo's Bar was half way along the front, separated from the sand by a cobbled track. The actual bar—which served tapas at weekends—was on the inside of the track, but it owned a concrete square, set under the pine trees, on the sea side and during the season tables and chairs were set out on this. Drinkers had the pleasure of a superb view—the large, semi-circular bay, the mountains which ringed it, the blue sky and even bluer sea, the yachts with their multi-coloured sails, and the topless sunbathers.

Evans traced a pattern in the frosting on his glass. 'A friend of mine's arriving at the end of the week. Mike's a yachtsman who's really only happy when he's frightening himself silly in a hurricane, but most summers he goes soft and enjoys a cruise. I often go with him—Italy, the Greek islands: depends what time there is. I was wondering if you'd like to join in? Bring a friend along, of course. We'll have company.'

'It sounds great, but I'm returning home.'

Evans drank. He watched a long-legged red-head, waring a monokini which only an optimist would have described as adequate, walk along the sand, hips swinging, proudly conscious of the attention she was generating. 'As Mike always says, sun, sail, and sex in a slow swell are an unbeatable combination. So put off your return for a couple of months.'

'I doubt I'll have the chance. I've got to start earning a living.'

'Two months won't make any difference to that and it'll give you some memories to live on when the rain's pissing down twenty-four hours a day.'

'Right now, two months would make one hell of a difference.'

'Skint?'

'Not quite,' said Sterne tightly.

'I'll lend you a stake.'

'No, thanks.'

'You're a difficult bastard.' Evans laughed. 'Not just honest, but proud with it! You realize that if you don't pay Hugh what's not due to him, you could come cruising?'

'I'm paying him.'

'I know a brunette who could bring a dead man back to life.'

Sterne said nothing.

'Stubborn to boot! Well, thank God there are some honest, proud, stubborn people left in the world and not everyone's like me. Maybe there's hope for the human race yet.' He drained his glass. 'Right, let's move on. I thought we'd try El Pescador for some grub.'

Sterne was surprised. El Pescador was the most expensive restaurant in Cala Survas.

The restaurant was on the eastern harbour arm: the bar was downstairs and the tables above. The décor was in overpoweringly bad taste, but the view through the windows was of the bay and the food was nearly as good as the prices suggested it should be.

Evans said: 'This is one of the few places in Spain which serves decent sweets. The chocolate mousse is as smooth and rich as anything you'll get in France.'

Sterne wondered how often Evans ate here. And where did the money come from? 'I'll settle for that, then.'

Evans gave the order. 'And I think we'll have a bottle of bubbly with the pud . . .'

'I've about had enough to drink,' Sterne intervened.

'If you know that much, then you haven't.' Evans called the wine waiter across. 'A bottle of Castellblanch, brut.'

The champagne arrived in an ice bucket, the cork was removed with professional ease, and their glasses were filled.

Evans said: 'Here's luck to us and to hell with the rest of the world.' He drank, put his glass down on the table. 'I've been thinking, Angus . . .' He was interrupted by the table waiter who set their sweets in front of them.

The chocolate mousse was smooth, rich, and flavoured with a tangy taste which Sterne tentatively identified as a mixture of orange and lemon: the whipped cream on top had been laced with Cointreau.

'How about a cigar?' Evans asked.

'I don't, thanks.'

Evans ordered a cigar. When it arrived, he lit and smoked it in a strangely intense manner, as if savouring something of which he'd been deprived for a long time. 'As I started to say, I've been scratching my head to work out a way of helping you.'

'There's no need to bother.'

'Honest, stubborn, and not just proud, but very, very proud.'

'I didn't mean to be ungracious.'

'Forget it. For God's sake, if friends can't pull each other's leg once in a while . . . How are you getting back to England? Anything booked?'

'Not yet.' And nothing could be booked until Ralph sent the money.

'So how would you feel about a trip back where all expenses are paid? And a hundred and fifty quid bonus at the end?'

Sterne said nothing.

'A bloke I know came along with the proposition, but I'm too busy—got to make that cruise. But I'm wondering if it mightn't help you.'

'What kind of a trip?'

'Taking a car from here to England. And the expenses will be generous.'

'Why isn't the owner driving the car back?'

'It's all right, the car won't be hot or anything like that.'

'That doesn't really answer my question.'

'I'm not going to answer it, Angus, until you say whether or not you're interested.' He drew on the cigar, blew a smoke ring which shimmered as it slowly rose. 'No need to decide here and now. Think about it. But don't be too long.'

*

Sterne stood on the balcony of his studio room and stared along the road at the segment of bay which he could see: a shaft of moonlight across the water added a touch of poetry.

Evans, jokingly, had called him a very proud man. If the wish to be independent was to be proud, then he was . . . When his parents had died, they'd left a considerable amount of capital which his uncle, one of the trustees of the trust set up by their will, had invested with great acumen so that the value of the trust had, over the years, considerably increased. It had been a complicated trust, aimed at making certain neither Ralph nor he came into the capital too young: his parents had been quite certain that too much money too soon ruined any man. When Ralph had reached 28 the original trust was broken and Ralph's share had vested absolutely, but his own share had become the subject of a fresh trust, of which Ralph was a trustee. (Perhaps right from the bcginning his parents had identified the streak of reckless adventure in him, just as they'd identified the conservative, cautious approach to life Ralph would always take.) Inevitably, Ralph had done all he could to suggest that his income from the new trust be spent wisely and with a view to the future, but all the time it was his money he'd felt he'd a perfect right to use it in the pursuit of living. Now, however, he needed more money to get him home and Ralph had told him a month before that there'd be no further income from the trust for three months, so he'd be asking Ralph to lend him money, not hand over what, subject to Ralph's approval (and Angela's disapproval), was legally his. His pride balked at the necessity . . .

He'd heard of people being offered a trip back to the UK by car in return for driving the car there, or sharing the driving, but in such cases it was normal for people to have to meet their own hotel and other expenses. Yet

Evans had said that not only would all expenses be paid on a generous scale (the implication being that there was profit to be made here), there would also be a hundred and fifty pounds at the end . . .

Evans had also called him honest. He was. Which meant that he was honest enough to acknowledge the fact that 'honesty' was a word which could not always be defined by the same set of standards. What if this proposed drive was in some respect an unusual one, but there was nothing inherently illegal about it . . . ?

CHAPTER 3

Evans's flat was on the top floor of one of the front apartment blocks. On the rooftop patio, four chairs were set round a cane table and Sterne stared out at the bay and saw a large yacht, having just cleared the harbour, break out her multi-coloured spinnaker. It reminded him of the cruise Evans had proposed: days of sun, nights of love . . .

Evans, who'd left to get the drinks, returned carrying a tray on which were two glasses and a bottle of champagne. He held the cork and twisted the bottle around it: the cork came free. He filled the two glasses and placed the bottle under the table in such shade as there was. 'The one advantage of this heat is that you have to drink quickly in order to prevent the champagne in the bottle becoming warm.'

'There is an alternative—put the bottle back in the fridge.'

'And waste good drinking time getting there and back?'

He was being judged, Sterne suddenly thought. But why and for what?

Evans offered a pack of Lambert and Butler cigarettes and, when Sterne shook his head, lit one.

'I've been thinking about what you mentioned yesterday,' Sterne said abruptly. 'It can't possibly be as simple as you made out.'

'Why not?'

'The offer's too generous.'

'A cynical approach. I'm delighted. There's hope yet that you'll survive in this shark-infested world . . .'

'If you're not prepared to be serious, forget it.'

'Hang on. I'm only being a bit facetious.' Evans studied Sterne. 'Things must be a lot tighter than you let on. So why in hell did you pay the extra sixty-five thousand over and above what you needed to? . . . Still, that's past history. And now you want to know why someone's willing to pay over the odds to have a car driven back to the UK. All right, I'll tell you. How much d'you know about the machinations of the Common Market?'

'No more than the next man.'

'In other words, the whole thing is just a sour joke . . . So you wouldn't know what the regulations are concerning the importation of used cars, with special reference to the reimportation of a car into its country of origin?'

'You're right—I wouldn't.'

'Suppose you're an Englishman who's fed up with the English weather and you decide to live abroad. Initially, you take your British registered car on which all proper taxes were paid when it was first bought. You settle in a Common Market country. Then, after a bit, you decide to get rid of the right-hand drive car and buy a left-hand, locally produced one. No native of your new country is going to, or probably is allowed to, buy it, so you've the option of driving it back to sell it yourself or finding a returning Englishman who'll take it from you or buy it on the spot. You're lucky. You find someone who buys it and gives a fair price and he drives off. When he reaches Britain the odds are the car no longer has a current excise licence so he declares himself to the Customs and explains what's happened. Their first question is—where did he buy the car. He tells 'em—France. Fine, they say, fill in this and that form, here's our certification that you've made all the proper declarations in case you should be stopped by a copper for not displaying the appropriate tax disc, and welcome back to a civilized country. But now let's change the scenario. He tells 'em he bought the car in Spain. They shake their heads. Spain wasn't in the Common Market when he bought the car so now he's got to pay taxes on importing it.'

'You said it was British built and all the taxes due had originally been paid.'

'Right.'

'Then there can't be anything to pay on its return into Britain.'

'Wrong. Under the Common Market regulations, there are—quite heavy ones in the case of a luxury car . . . Have some more champagne to help overcome the shock of discovering the depths to which the bureaucratic mind can sink.'

Evans refilled their glasses. 'You'll have the picture by now. The people with luxury cars are the rich tax exiles who mustn't return to the UK until they've established beyond any shadow of a doubt that they're ordinarily non-resident in the UK for tax purposes. Someone like that can't just drive his car back. That seems to leave him with only two choices. One, he can pay someone to drive it back and sell it for him—but being very rich he expects to be swindled at every turn: two, he can sell it locally, but only at the kind of discount which gives him ulcers. That's why a bit of trade's sprung up—a trade which gives him a third option.

'A third party comes along and makes an offer for the car that's less than he'd get in the UK, but more than he could hope for from a local sale. He doesn't like the money being less than it would be in the UK, of course—

the rich are the only people left who still count their pennies—but he's paid in the local currency and cash always soothes.

'As for the third party, he has the car driven back to the UK where it's sold for the market price, so he's in pocket.'

'How can he be if the car has to pay the Common Market tax on re-entry into the UK?'

'That's an interesting question.'

'Then what's the answer?'

'It enters the UK with papers proving that it was bought in France and is therefore not liable to the tax.'

'Fakes?'

'If a bunch of clowns think up such bloody stupid rules and regulations, what else can they expect? . . . How'd you like to take a car back?'

Sterne hesitated, then said: 'I need to think about it.'

'Sure. But things are a bit sharper than I thought they were and I'll need the answer inside twenty-four hours. A car's turned up, so the sooner it's in the UK, the sooner the capital's back in circulation.'

The red Mercedes 380SEL might have come out of the showrooms the previous day: the registration number said it was a year old.

'Mercedes are all right,' said Evans, as he stared at the parked car, 'but give me a Porsche. I had a turbo nine-eleven not so long back. Put my foot down and every other car on the road started going backwards.'

'What about papers?' Sterne asked.

'They're all in the glove locker.'

'And what happens after I cross the border?'

'Let's go up to the flat so I can give you the details.'

They took the lift up to the sixth floor. In the large sitting-room, which offered the same uninterrupted view of the bay as the patio above, Evans crossed to an occasional table made from a section of very ancient, gnarled olive wood. He spread out a map. 'D'you know the roads through to France?'

'Only vaguely.'

'If I were you, I'd stick to the motorway as that's the easiest and quickest route to the border. Once in France, make for Lençon and aim to be there by Friday evening. Lençon's here.' Evans used his long forefinger to indicate a town in the Lot et Garonne department. 'Leave the town on the Bergerac road and keep going for eight kilometres until you come to the Trois Etoiles motel. A room will be reserved for you. Don't be misled into thinking the grub's good there. When you want to eat return to Lençon and go to the Bourgogne. And if you'll take my advice, you'll start with their truffle omelette.

'On Saturday morning you'll be contacted and handed fresh papers for the car, proving you bought it in France—a notorized letter of sale, insurance green card . . . the usual bumph.'

'And then?'

'Lençon will tell you where to take the car in the UK.'

'What if something goes wrong?'

Evans laughed. 'No need to get your knickers in a twist. Nothing'll go wrong.'

It was unlike Sterne to worry, but the knowledge that he'd be breaking the law left him feeling on edge, even though he could be certain that few people would censure him for breaking so ridiculous and inequitable a law as this one.

Evans stood upright. 'That leaves just one thing. Expenses.' He picked up an envelope. 'There's five hundred dollars in here, in dollars and francs.'

Sterne took the envelope and pushed it into his trouser pocket.

'Aren't you going to check it's all there?'

'No.'

Evans looked quizzically at him. 'You'll never stay rich.'

'That's a sure bet.'

'Have a good trip, then. And don't forget, the Bourgogne. Their truffle omelette will tell you why the French all have bad livers by the time they're forty.'

Sterne stood on the balcony of his studio room and stared along the road at the bay. The cynics said, never return. So perhaps he'd never return to Cala Survas, but it was a sad thought despite the concrete developments, package-tour amenities, memento shops, and Sonia's Levantine.

He returned into the room, picked up his suitcase, and left. The landlady was waiting on the ground floor and she kissed him on both cheeks and told him that he was like a son to her and his going away was breaking her heart. Her grief was genuine—she came of an emotional people. Additionally, a number of flats in the town had not been let this season because of a slight decrease in the number of tourists and she might not find another tenant by September.

He left the house and went over to the Mercedes, put the suitcase on the back seat, and settled behind the wheel. To reach the nearest access point on the motorway, sixteen kilometres away, he needed to drive towards the west and then turn inland: he drove to the east. He wasn't a fool and knew that cars were used for smuggling and he judged, not least from the certainty with which Evans had said that he'd not have paid Smedley the full bet, that Evans would never hesitate to take advantage of someone if it would be to his financial advantage.

The one-man garage stood on the outskirts of the town, next to a section where an apartment block had been begun but then the finances had failed. Fernando, the owner, was an ardent windsurfer, which was how Sterne had come to know him. He was working on the engine of an old and very battered Seat 600.

'Can you do something for me?' Sterne asked in his workable Spanish.

Fernando straightened up. 'Anything to get away from this old pig of a car.' He rubbed the small of his back. 'What's the trouble?' He moved to his left to look through the opened doorway of his garage. 'That's not your job, there?'

'Temporarily, yes.'

Fernando whistled through gapped teeth. 'Hell, man, that's a specialist's job. You need the agents in Barcelona.'

'There's nothing wrong mechanically. I want you to check whether anything's hidden in it.'

Fernando spoke curiously. 'What kind of anything?'

'I don't know. Just something that shouldn't be there.'

'It'll take time. There's an amazing number of places in the car you can hide things.'

'It doesn't matter how long. I just want to be certain the car's clean.'

'OK. Give me a hand to push this old pig out of the way.' He reached out and slapped the Seat 600 with the palm of his hand. 'When we've done that, drive the Mercedes over the pit.'

Two and a half hours later—half an hour of which had been spent in the nearest bar—Fernando reflated the spare tyre and secured it in position. 'That's it, then. Nothing.'

'Thanks a lot. What do I owe you?'

'Nothing. It's a goodbye present.'

Sterne knew enough about the Spanish character not to argue. Instead, he drove to the nearest shop and bought a dozen bottles of 103 brandy. He presented these as his goodbye present. Fernando insisted on opening one of the bottles to make certain the contents were all that they should be.

Sterne left Cala Survas, heading westwards, at twenty

past one. He switched on the radio and tuned in to the Barcelona station which played classical music all day. Plácido Domingo was singing an aria from *Rigoletto*. He joined in.

CHAPTER 4

The rain, which had started minutes before, came down with near-tropical intensity and sections of the road were awash: even on fast speed, the wipers of the Mercedes couldn't keep the windscreen clear and the world beyond was distorted. Sterne slowed still further, thankful the bumpy road was virtually deserted and he wasn't faced with French drivers who regarded natural hazards as a reason for increasing speed: then he cursed because he shouldn't ever have been on this road, passing through a waterlogged, bleak countryside in which he had seen no sign of habitation for several kilometres. He wondered where in the hell he'd taken the wrong turning.

Through the streaming windscreen, he saw that the road forked and there was a signpost. Lençon to the right, 15 kilometres. He swore again. Half an hour ago, Lençon had been 18 kilometres away. He must have been driving in a semi-circle.

The intensity of the rain increased, although up to now he'd have said that that was impossible, and it was because he slowed still further that he caught sight of the figure, sheltering under an evergreen oak. He braked to a stop, partially lowered the passenger window, and in schoolboy French called to know if he could offer a lift.

There was no response. He decided his voice could not have carried against the drumming of the rain and he shouted at the top of his voice.

The person finally moved and he identified her as a

woman. She walked, clutching her blouse with one hand, with an uneven step. She stopped when half way to the car, careless of the rain, staring at him with a look which even through the torrential downpour he could identify as one of fright.

'Mademoiselle, what is the trouble? Come to the car and I will help.'

She hesitated, then came forward once more. Her foot caught on something and she almost fell and instinctively let go of the blouse and held both hands to brace herself. He saw that her sodden blouse was torn.

He pushed open the car door.

'Who's in the car?' she demanded, in English.

'I'm on my own. Look, whatever the trouble is, I'm sure I can help.'

The rain plastered her torn blouse and jeans to her body as she stared at him, desperately trying to reach a decision.

'I promise you'll be safe.'

She climbed in and he realized the reason for her hoppity motion was that she was wearing only one shoe. He turned to reach over the seat to the back and she flinched away from him. 'My suitcase is on the back seat and there's a towel in it: that'll mop up a little of the wet.' Careful to move no closer to her, he opened the suitcase and brought out the towel which he handed to her. 'I'll turn the heater on full. I don't know if I can direct all the air your way, but I'll try . . . Why not take off a few of your wet things . . .'

'Oh Christ!' she cried as she reached for the door-handle.

'What's the matter?'

'You're trying . . .'

'I'm trying to find the quickest way of getting you dry.'

Slowly she let go of the door handle. 'I'll stay wet.'

'Well, at least dry yourself as much as possible with the towel.'

As he switched on the heater and set the controls to give the maximum amount of hot air, she used the towel to mop herself. It was impossible for her to do this without letting go of the torn blouse. He looked away.

After a while she said: 'Have you got a cigarette?'

'I'm afraid not. I don't smoke.'

'God!' She began to sob, deep retching sobs which made her body shake.

'Can you tell me what happened? Has someone hurt you?'

'They tried to rape me,' she answered, her voice shrill. 'What is it—d'you want all the filthy details?'

'I just want to do the best I can to help. We'll drive straight to Lençon where I'll buy you some cigarettes and then take you to the police . . .'

'The police? Ask a French policeman what rape is and he'll tell you it's when a woman has second thoughts.'

'But they can call a doctor . . .'

'And can he wash away the memory?'

'Were you physically injured?'

'No.'

He released the handbrake and accelerated slowly away, into the torrent of rain which drummed so hard on the car's roof that he had almost to shout. 'When we reach the town who can I get in touch with? I could phone England . . .'

'No.'

'Surely there's someone . . .'

'No.'

He deemed it best not to argue any further for the moment.

As they entered Lençon, the rain becan to ease. He braked to a halt outside a tobacconist. 'What kind of cigarettes d'you like?'

'Any.'

He ran into the tobacconist. The woman behind the counter had the cantankerousness of old age and she seemed determined not to understand his halting French, but eventually, with the aid of much gesticulating, he managed to make her realize that he wanted some cigarettes, it didn't matter what brand, and some matches. She sold him a pack of John Player Specials which, being imported, were the most expensive she had in stock.

Back in the car, he handed them to his passenger and she lit one.

'Would it be an idea to introduce ourselves?' he asked. 'I'm Angus Sterne.'

She said nothing, but went on smoking. The interior of the car was very hot and she had begun to dry: she'd somehow managed to secure the blouse so that she no longer had to hold it closed.

'I don't know whether to call you Agatha or Zenobia?'

There was a long pause before she said: 'Belinda.'

'Belinda what?'

An even longer pause. 'Backman.'

'Don't you think it would be a good idea to see the police now and explain what happened?'

'I told you, I'm not seeing them.'

'All right. Then we'll try and find a doctor . . .'

'Can't you understand?' Her voice rose. 'I won't see anyone.'

'If you're certain?'

'Yes.'

'Look, I'm booked in at a motel just north of here. Let's go straight there after . . .'

'You can forget that,' she said contemptuously.

'What I was going to suggest,' he said, in the same even tone, 'was that you book in there for the night in a separate cabin after you've bought some clothes.'

'What do I use for money?'

It occurred to him for the first time that she had with her only the clothes she was wearing. 'I'll take care of that.'

'Like hell you will.'

'Is there any way I can convince you I'm only trying to help, not seduce, you?'

She turned and stared straight at him: her expression was one of suspicion, yet also of frightened hope.

'I've been in one or two tight corners and each time I've been hellish lucky and there's been someone around to help. So I know how desperately one can need that help. If I buy you clothes, take you out for a meal, and pay for the motel, I will not be looking for repayment in bed, or anywhere else.'

'You . . . you swear that?'

'Cross my heart and hope to die.'

For the first time since she'd entered the car, she relaxed slightly. 'Don't do that until you've bought me something to wear so I look less like a drowned rat.'

The Bourgogne was in the centre of Lençon, overlooking the main square. Its décor was dull, even dowdy, but it was patronized by a number of Frenchmen, many with their families, which was a more certain guide to the standard of its cuisine.

Belinda and Sterne were shown to one of the corner tables, from which they could look out at the square. The menus were brought and once they decided what to eat he started to order, inevitably having difficulty in pronouncing some of the words. Belinda took over, showing that she spoke the language fluently.

The omelettes truffés were as good as Evans had promised they would be, the veau Orloff equally delicious, the tartelettes cœur à la crème a miraculous mélange of cream cheese, sugar, cream, strawberries, and redcurrant jelly.

The waiter brought them coffee and two Bisquits. They warmed the glasses in their hands. 'It's strange, isn't it, how tiny things can alter one's life in such a big way,' she said, her voice low, her thoughts far away. 'Something which at the time doesn't seem it could possibly be of any consequence whatsoever turns out to be vitally important.' She sipped the cognac. 'But for that red dress . . .'

'A red dress?' he prompted.

'It was in a little shop at the back of the town, somewhere where you'd never have expected to find anything so chic. I tried it on and it was exactly me: and I remembered how Jean had told me I should wear red more often because it made me glow and I wanted to show him I'd remembered . . . I'd just enough money left to buy it, but then I couldn't get a train ticket . . . I bought the dress and the woman wrapped it up as if it had been an Emmanuel Ungaro. I wasn't worried about the train ticket. I'd been hitch-hiking for a couple of months and nothing had ever happened.' She put the glass down, lit a cigarette. 'Do you want to hear the beastly details?'

'Only if you want to tell them to me.'

'Maybe sharing them will distance them a bit . . . The first car that stopped for me had a French family. Very typical. Father with a belly, mother who agreed with everything he said and then did what she wanted, and two rowdy kids. They were turning off at Echaux so they dropped me there. The kids had been making such a racket I was glad to see them go . . .

'Along came this blood-red Mondial Quattrovalve. The two men in it were smooth. Where was I trying to get to? What a coincidence—that's where they were passing through. There was just enough room in the back since it was a two plus two so they hoped I wouldn't feel cramped. Did I like driving fast? . . . Christ, could he drive!

Frightened me, yet at the same time excited me. As a matter of fact, I don't suppose he was ever actually in danger of hitting anyone, but he liked the thrill of taking risks . . . I suppose that's really why they made their play for me. Anyone with their sort of money is never hard up for women ten times smarter than me, but then it's all too easy and there's no risk . . . They said we'd have a picnic lunch. We stopped in Betaneau and they bought foie gras and a couple of bottles of Mouton Rothschild. Their kind don't know that you can picnic on cheese and vin ordinaire. When we left there we took the road which crosses the Etaples Plateau and half way across, in the middle of nowhere, they decided to stop.' She finished the cognac and stared down into the glass.

Sterne caught a waiter's attention and pointed to the glass. The wine waiter came across with a bottle and refilled both glasses.

She lit a cigarette. 'They drank the wine as if it had been the crudest of crude vin ordinaire and when they'd finished the second bottle they started on me. There was no attempt to find out if I was likely to be cooperative. They wanted rape. I tell you, they wanted rape.'

He reached out and put his hand on hers, resting on the table. He half-expected her to snatch her hand away, but she did nothing for quite a while before sliding it free, making it a casual act without any significance.

'The place was littered with stones and I managed to get hold of one the size of my fist and I slammed it down on the nearer head. That kept him quiet for a bit. The other man didn't like that—no objection to hurting others, bloody scared of being hurt—so I had the chance to break free and run. I suppose they'd have caught me if it hadn't suddenly rained like the second flood was starting just as I reached a wood.'

'Thank God it rained and you found that wood.'

'Yes,' she murmured. 'Thank God.'

*

The motel consisted of offices and a restaurant and three lines of cabins. Sterne drove slowly along the last line and then stopped. 'Here we are—number fourteen. You've got the key?'

'Yes,' Belinda answered, her voice high.

He spoke easily, as if unaware of the fact that she had shown an increasing tension from the moment they'd left the restaurant. 'I'd see you to the cabin door, but the agreement is, I stay here.'

She climbed out, shut the door, adjusted the collar of her coat against the rain which had eased until it was now little more than a light drizzle. She took a pace up the very short path, stopped, and turned. He lowered the window. 'Have you forgotten something?"

'To thank you for everything.'

'There's no need.'

She stared at him and he thought she was going to break down and cry once more, but then she controlled her emotions. 'Good night, Angus.' She went up to the front door, unlocked it, and entered the cabin.

He backed the car to a point where he could turn, carried on round to the front row and cabin number 40.

Five minutes later he sat in an armchair beyond twin single beds, tired but not yet ready to get into bed. Tomorrow morning someone would contact him and hand him the new papers for the Mercedes. Then it was back to England and the routine of the prosaic life of a man who had to learn to earn a living . . .

His mind drifted. How could Belinda have been so naive as to believe she could go on hitch-hiking without meeting trouble? She wasn't beautiful, in the sense of lush, hot-house perfection, but she certainly had the piquant attractiveness which came from slight imperfections: curly brown hair which wouldn't stay in place but danced around, an oval face that had a very slight bias to one side, blue eyes too large, a snub nose, cheerful lips too generous, a body a shade too rounded for contemporary beanstalk tastes. She must have known how men were always looking at her. Yet at the beginning she had just seen the two Italians as sophisticated, friendly, a little inclined to show off. She was too trusting: too ready to believe in other people's good nature . . .

CHAPTER 5

Next morning Sterne left his cabin at half past eight to make his way to the restaurant, where he found he was the only guest present. He sat at one of the window tables and a waitress brought him two croissants, butter, apricot jam, and coffee. He was eating the second croissant when a middle-aged woman, plump, dowdy, with thick horn-rimmed spectacles which were the wrong style for her square, heavy face, entered the restaurant and crossed to his table. 'Monsieur Sterne?' Her husky voice held a thick accent, often making it difficult immediately to understand her words.

He came to his feet. 'Have a seat.' As she sat, he noticed that the lines around her eyes and the sagging flesh on her neck suggested that she was older than he'd first judged. 'Will you have something to eat? Coffee?'

'No,' she replied curtly. 'Was the border crossing with no trouble?'

'Nobody was interested in either me or the car. I didn't even have to show the papers.'

'Where is the papers now?'

'In the car.'

'Get them.'

'Sure, just as soon as I've finished eating.' She reminded

him of the matron at his prep school. Old Battleaxe they'd called her, with all the cruelty of youth.

She was silent—her expression hadn't altered, but there was no doubting her resentment at this delay—until he'd finished the croissant, then she said: 'You will get them now.'

He didn't bother to object on the grounds that he hadn't finished his coffee. He left, went through to his cabin, returned with the papers, still in the envelope in which Evans had handed them to him.

She carefully checked through the papers, replacing them when she was satisfied. Then she opened her large, crocodile-skin handbag and brought out a second brown envelope, twin to the first. 'These are for England. Be certain everything is good.'

The first thing he noticed was that the car was now in his name. 'Aren't you taking a risk? With these I could sell the car and pocket the money.'

'Are you so stupid?'

He wondered if that was a straight question, an implied criticism, or a threat? He checked through the rest of the papers. 'Everything looks fine. So where do I go from here?'

'I am telling you,' she said sharply, annoyed that he should imagine he needed to ask. 'Drive as you wish, but you come to Calais for to take the seven-thirty boat on Monday evening.'

'This coming Monday?'

Her expression became impatient.

'I was hoping to drift around a bit in the Loire valley . . .'

'Monday evening. You drive to the motel in Newingreen which is close by . . . 'Ithe . . .'

'It's all right, I know Newingreen and Hythe well. My brother lives not all that far away . . .'

'A room is booked. Someone speaks to you and takes

the car. Is that certain?'

'Couldn't be more certain.'

'Very well.' She tugged at the collar of the printed cotton frock she was wearing, which would have looked charming on someone half her age and size.

'Now that business is concluded, will you change your mind and have a coffee?'

'I do not change my mind.'

He believed her. She stood. He did the same, smiled, and said goodbye. She nodded, then left. Old Battleaxe hadn't liked him either, he thought, as he watched her through the window and saw her stride across the forecourt. To his surprise, she unlocked the door of a BMW. He'd have placed her in a Renault 5.

Belinda, dressed in the clothes she'd bought the previous afternoon, yawned as she refilled her coffee cup.

He said: 'My mother used to say, the more you sleep, the tireder you become.'

'I just couldn't get to sleep—my mind was going round and round. Then when I did finally drop off, I crashed out. You really should have woken me up.'

'There's no rush.'

She looked out at the sunny forecourt. 'Thank God the rain's cleared. I was born for sun. If I had to live in somewhere like Sweden, I'd commit suicide.'

'You'd get used to it.'

She'd bought a small, cheap but attractive handbag the previous evening and from this she brought a pack of cigarettes. She lit one.

'By the way, Belinda, I don't know what your plans are, but I'm driving up to Calais, probably via Périgueux, Limoges, Chartres, and Rouen. If you'd care to come along, I can take you back to England.'

'I live here, in France.'

He was surprised, then realized that he shouldn't have

been since her French was so fluent. 'Whereabouts?'

'Not all that far from Chinon.'

'Isn't that fairly close to my route?'

'Yes.'

'Then I can drop you right on your doorstep. Why on earth didn't you let me ring your parents yesterday?'

Her mouth tightened.

'Sorry . . . I never did learn to mind my own business.'

'Don't be silly. It's me who's never learned . . .' She didn't finish.

He waited, then said: 'You're coming as far as Chinon, then?'

'If you'll put up with me?'

'I'm only sorry you don't live at Calais.'

She smiled.

'Tell you what. We'll buy some food for a picnic and . . .' He stopped.

She stubbed out the cigarette. 'There's no need to treat me like a shrinking Victorian violet.'

'It's just . . .'

'That was yesterday. This is today.'

'Sometimes associations hurt.'

'There aren't any.'

He wondered.

They drove through the village of Brillant at a quarter to five. As they passed the last of the shuttered houses, she broke the companionable silence which had lasted almost ten minutes. 'Do you like secret gorges?'

'I don't think I know any.'

'Then go right at the next crossroads.'

At the crossroads, he turned off the wide main road into a lane which ran dead straight up the rising land ahead of them until it became lost among trees.

'Jean—my stepfather—brought me here for the first time when I was just sixteen, seven years ago.'

He'd placed her as slightly older than 23: perhaps because the lines of fear had still not entirely gone.

'It was a day when I'd been even more obnoxious than usual.'

He smiled.

'I promise you that at sixteen I was nearly as obnoxious as I was hypocritical . . .' She became silent.

He did not break into her thoughts and they reached the wood and carried on through this to breast a rise, beyond which was a T-junction. 'Turn right,' she said.

'Into that lane?' he asked, judging how narrow it was.

'You'll get through. I've been along it in a Peugeot five-o-six and that's just as wide as this car.'

He slowed to a crawl and turned right. Soon, the lane was bordered by high earth banks.

'Jean brought me here on my sixteenth birthday after I'd been very rude to him,' she said suddenly.

'Why were you rude?'

'To begin with, I hated him for all the usual reasons—but also, I think I was just a little bit afraid of him. I seemed to see in him someone strong and able to be cruel . . . But in fact he's one of the kindest men: at least to Evelyn, my mother, and me. Anyway, he could so easily have told me a few home truths, but he didn't. Instead, he brought me here to the secret gorge where he'd always come when he'd been young and in trouble. He said it was so peaceful that after a little while everything in his mind began to sort itself out because there wasn't any longer any room for things like envy and hate. Of course, I just sneered: at sixteen I knew much better than to go for that sort of sentimental claptrap. And in any case, if he said something was white, I knew it was black.

'The funny thing was, when we reached the gorge I couldn't, try as I did, stop myself beginning to think that perhaps life wasn't so terrible, I wasn't born to a malign fate, and Jean wasn't an ogre.'

The lane made a very sharp left turn and to get round this he had to reduce speed to a walking pace. Once round, the trees thinned and then there were open fields, rising on either side, in which sheep grazed. The lane continued to climb, more slowly, for half a kilometre.

'I hope nothing's coming in the opposite direction,' he said. 'We've not passed a turning point and I'd hate to have to back all the way.'

'There won't be anyone. I told you, this is a secret gorge.'

The lane curved right and abruptly ended at a miniature plateau. He stopped the car. Below them was the gorge, not deep or rugged enough to be dramatic, but a place of soft, gentle beauty: at the bottom, a river ran wide and slowly.

They left the car and walked along a rough, natural, zigzagging path until they were two-thirds of the way down and there they sat. Two swallowtails fluttered by; several crag martins swooped and wheeled; a pigeon planed in and then, with one quick clap of wings, landed in an oak tree; a wren began to sing.

He watched her face and saw the peace relax her. He closed his eyes and let his own mind drift . . .

'I should have come here when it first blew up,' she said. 'Maybe then I'd have seen sense.'

He'd been nearing sleep and her initial words startled him.

'I knew at the time that that's what I ought to do, but I wouldn't because then I'd maybe realize how stupid I was being. I don't suppose you can begin to understand the logic of that.' She picked up some small stones and let them trickle back on to the ground. 'Jean's the kind of person who doesn't mind coming straight out with what he thinks and he said that Michel was nothing but a rotter. That hurt my pride so I tried my damnedest to hurt him. I said that the only reason he talked like that was that he was jealous of Michel. Twenty-three and just as much a bloody fool as at sixteen: as if I hadn't learned over and over again that Jean loved me as a daughter and in no other way. My mother was angrier than I'd ever seen her before because she was so afraid that Jean would be really upset and hurt. But he knows far too much about the world to be hurt by such stupidity. What hurts him is when someone he loves is heading for trouble and he can't get them to realize it . . .

'I suppose one of the reasons I fell for Michel was the hint of viciousness. There's often some strange attraction to playing with fire. And I'd convinced myself that underneath the surface was an ordinarily decent man and I could bring that part of him to life . . . Women are suckers for saints.

'I'd always had money and Michel obviously thought I'd a fortune in my own right. When he discovered that most of the money came from Jean he told me to write and ask him for money. Jean refused to send any, so Michel wanted me to write again, saying we were living in appalling conditions and I was ill and couldn't afford a doctor . . . With all his sharpness, he couldn't realize it would be patently obvious who'd composed that letter.

'It was then that I finally accepted what kind of a man Michel really was and decided to leave him. I could have just disappeared, but I've never liked doing things the coward's way, so I told him. First he tried to bully me into changing my mind, then he started hitting me. I just managed to escape a bad beating-up . . . After that, I couldn't get home quickly enough to tell Jean something he didn't need telling—that he'd been quite right. But I fell in love with a red frock and there was a Ferrari with two Italians in it . . .'

She was silent for a while, then she said: 'Shall we move?'

He said nothing, but was surprised by this sudden suggestion.

As they drove back on to the main road, he said: 'Where do we go from here?'

'Go?' she said, her thoughts obviously miles away.

'Which way do I drive to reach your place?'

'But . . .'

'But what?'

'Nothing . . . Keep going along this road until I say.'

They passed through an undulating countryside, mainly given over to corn-growing and stock-grazing although there were a few vineyards. They passed through Bruyinal, a small town noted for its gem of a gothic church, and left on the Chinon road. They had just reached the outskirts of the village of Vertagne when she said: 'Stop here.'

He braked. 'Is something up?'

'No.'

He looked through the windscreen at the small, drab house just this side of a sharp bend. 'You live here?'

'No. But I'm leaving you here.'

A lorry, easing its way round the bend and past them, drowned some of her words. 'What did you say?'

'I'm leaving you here, Angus. So it's a case of trying to say thank you . . .'

'It's a case of explaining why I'm dropping you here instead of at your home.'

'Because . . .'

'Is that the answer?'

'Oh God, you're making it difficult for me.'

'All I'm asking for is an answer.'

'You've been so wonderful to me and I owe you more than I can ever repay, but . . .'

'But what?'

'Please, won't you just accept things as they are?'

'I can't,' he said bluntly.

'Oh God, why does life have to become so complicated?'

'What are you finding it so difficult to say? That you don't want me to know where you live so you don't have to see me again?'

'It's not really like that.'

'Then what is it really like?'

There was a quick squeal of brakes and he automatically looked up to see a blue Rover which had just come round the bend. The two men in it had obviously been surprised by something and he imagined there must have been a dog or cat which had run across the road. The car passed them. 'Do you want to see me again?' he asked.

'I . . . I can't answer you . . . D'you know we've seen that car three times today?'

'Really. Why can't you answer me?'

'It's got the same registration letters as my initials.'

'I don't give a damn if it's got HRH. Why can't you say if you do or don't want to see me again?'

'Each time it's been going in a different direction from us.'

'Belinda, for God's sake, forget that bloody car, even if it's got six wheels. You told me earlier on you weren't a coward and you always tried to say what you had to. So now tell me, do you want to see me again or am I suffering from a bad case of BO?'

'I don't know what I want,' she said despairingly, 'and that's what's so terrible, after all you've done for me. But the truth is . . .' She swallowed heavily.

As he saw her distress, his disappointment and pique gave way to compassion. 'It's all right. You've got reasons and they're yours and no business of mine.'

'They are your business after what you've done for me. But I just don't know if I can explain without hurting you . . . I've always thought of myself as being reasonably tough-minded, but after those two men had tried to rape me I was so terrified I just couldn't pull myself together. And last night, when I finally did get to sleep, my dreams were so awful that when I awoke I couldn't, for a long time, find the courage to get out of bed . . . I hoped a visit to the secret gorge would make things better, but maybe even that can't work miracles quickly. So yesterday's still a nightmare and although it was you who saved me from it, you're . . . you're a part of it. When I look at you, I keep remembering . . . Angus, I've got to be away from you before I can find out if I can separate you from the nightmare . . . Can you begin to understand?'

'I think so,' he answered, unable to suggest that this was easy.

She reached up and touched his arm with brief, but unmistakable gratitude. 'D'you mind if I go now?'

'Mind?' He hesitated, then altered what he'd been going to say. 'No, of course not. But you can't just disappear like that. You've no money for a taxi to get you to your place.' He produced some notes.

'All I need is enough for a phone call.'

'Take this.' He held out a ten-franc note.

'Just give me a couple of francs.'

'Look . . .'

'Just a couple of francs,' she repeated, her voice strained.

He replaced the notes in his pocket and brought out some change. He handed her two one-franc pieces. 'There's something more you've forgotten.'

'What?'

'When you've finally decided we can meet again, how are you going to let me know? . . . I'll give you my address in the UK.' He wrote Ralph's address and telephone number down on a piece of paper. 'Guard this well.'

She managed a brief, strained smile. 'That's a promise.' She turned and opened the door. He climbed out and came round to the pavement. 'Goodbye, good luck, and an early end to nightmares.'

'Oh, Angus, if only to God I could be sensible and see things differently . . .' She came forward and kissed him on the cheek. 'Please go quickly,' she whispered.

As he drove towards the corner, he looked in the rear-view mirror. He saw the slim figure in red and white still standing where he'd left her, and he felt lonely.

CHAPTER 6

He crossed the Channel on Sunday night, on the 7.30 ferry, having driven the last hundred kilometres at a speed which should have resulted in half a dozen speeding tickets. Calais had been enjoying late sunshine, Dover was suffering cloud and the air had the damp promise of rain.

The tempers of returning motorists were not improved when it became obvious that the Customs officers were carrying out an extensive search on every car.

'For God's sake, what the hell are they after?' asked a man who was nearly bald, but had a luxuriant moustache.

'Whatever they can find,' replied Sterne, as they stood by the side of the Fiesta in which the man's wife was trying to pacify two small and very tired children.

'Nobody's moved for ten minutes now. But I've got to make Reading tonight and be back at work tomorrow morning.'

'We shouldn't be long now.'

'It's too bloody long, whatever. D'you hear 'em?' He jerked his head in the direction of the car in which the two children were now crying. 'I said to the lady wife, leave the kids with Granny and let's have a proper holiday. She wouldn't. Women are driven crazy by their kids, but when they get the chance to dump 'em, they won't. Funny, isn't it?'

'I've no experience in the matter.'

'Then you're lucky and if you'll take my advice you'll see you stay that way.'

A seagull passed overhead and left behind a greeting which splattered the roof of the Fiesta.

'And the same to you,' shouted the man at the departing bird. He fiddled with his moustache. 'You wouldn't know if the Customs are opening bottles, would you?'

'I wouldn't, no.'

'Shouldn't think they would be. Only . . . only they're taking their time, aren't they?'

'Worried?'

'In a manner of speaking.' He lowered his voice and looked around: had any official been nearby his attention would immediately have been caught by the man's attempts to preserve secrecy. 'A pal put me up to it. You buy some of those plastic bottles of mineral water, remove the caps very carefully, empty out the water and fill with gin. Then you replace the caps and glue 'em down so it looks as if they've never been touched. Only what the hell do I do if they start poking around too hard and begin to wonder what I'm doing bringing water back to England after a summer when it's never stopped raining?'

'Tell 'em you've got bad kidneys and this particular mineral water does them a power of good.'

'You think they'll wear that?'

'What have you got to lose?'

'I suppose . . . It'd be just my luck to get clobbered. My wife says I'm a born loser.'

'In that case, try a policy of complete honesty.'

'What? Admit the bottles all contain gin?'

'The word "complete" is qualified. Forget the gin, but list everything else in the car, right down to the stale sandwiches. That'll give the appearance of naivety which always fixes the Customs.'

The man looked at Sterne uncertainly, but at that moment the line of cars began to move and he hurriedly climbed into the Fiesta.

Sterne returned to the Mercedes and drove forward, to be brought to a halt by a single-pole barrier. It was, he thought, as he switched off the engine, a pity he couldn't treat his own case as lightly as he had the other man's. He was becoming more and more aware of the fact that the car's papers were false . . .

The single pole lifted and he restarted the engine. Small chequered bollards had been used to map out two tracks across the concrete apron and these wheeled round, out of sight of the waiting cars, to two wooden huts, one on either side of a central barrier of hardboard nailed on to a wooden frame.

A Customs officer—young, hard-faced, coldly polite—said: 'Would you take your luggage in to the hut, please. And make certain you leave the boot unlocked.'

He carried his single suitcase and plastic shopping-bag of presents into the hut. The Customs officer followed and carefully shut the door so that the car was no longer visible, then went behind a trestle-table which, except for two institutional wooden chairs, was the only furniture. 'Put your things down on here, please.'

Sterne set the suitcase and bag on the table. The Customs officer picked up a clipboard on which was a single printed page and held this out. 'Please read the regulations concerning the importation of goods and chattels brought abroad . . .'

'Thanks, but I know 'em.'

The Customs officer put the clipboard down on the trestle table. 'Your passport, please.'

Sterne handed this over.

'You're quite certain, Mr. Sterne, that you do

understand that you have to declare everything you've brought abroad or aboard the ship?'

'Yes, I am. The suitcase is full of clothes. A couple of the T-shirts were bought in France some months ago, the rest of the stuff comes from this country. In the plastic shopping-bag are a bottle of whisky, two bottles of red wine, a small bottle of very expensive scent, and a doll which walks and talks and needs its nappies changed after you've pressed its tummy.'

The Customs officer did not smile. He handed the passport back, pressed the catches of the suitcase to open the lid: 'Where have you come from?'

'Cagnes. That's a little place a bit back from the sea. Renoir once lived and worked there . . .'

'I do know it.'

Sterne realized he was talking too much. Would he now be asked for the car's papers . . .

The door of the shed opened and a second Customs officer, with two gold rings on the sleeves of his reefer jacket, entered. A considerably older man, his craggy face possessed lines of tolerance and good humour. 'Is everything going all right?' It was not until later that Sterne realized that the words had been a coded message.

The first man nodded. 'We're trying to move things as quickly as we can.'

'Good.' The second man turned to Sterne; 'Sorry about this delay. I know just how frustrating it must be. The holiday's over and all you want to do is get back home, but here we are, holding everything up. Doesn't take us very far up the popularity charts, does it?'

Sterne smiled. 'I'm afraid your job probably keeps you out of those altogether.'

'Oh, well, I suppose I could find some consolation in the fact that someone has to do the job . . . Nearly finished, Basil?'

'Just about, sir.' The first man closed the lid of the suitcase.

Reassured by the senior man's friendliness, Sterne said: 'Is something up that you're carrying out a search of all the cars?'

'Nothing special. But now and then we have to have a bit of a blitz, just to remind everyone that it can happen. You know how some people are. Unless they reckon there could be a stiff search, they'll try and import a whole brewery.'

'That's all right, then, Mr Sterne,' said the younger Customs officer, still very correct and showing none of the friendliness of his superior.

Sterne left the hut and returned to the car. He settled behind the wheel, switched on the engine, and engaged drive. The further pole barrier lifted.

He drove to Folkestone and then cut through the back of the town to continue on the A20, ignoring the quicker motorway. At Newingreen, he turned into the forecourt of the motel. It would take at least a couple of good stiff drinks to remove the effects of the tension he'd suffered back in Dover.

Sterne looked at his watch for the third time in under a quarter of an hour. Twenty past two and still no one had contacted him. He thought back to Lençon and recalled what the woman had said. Someone would be in touch with him at the motel in Newingreen. So had something gone wrong with their arrangements?

He left the building and stood out in the weak sun and stared at the Mercedes which he'd had to move from the cabin's garage before noon. Did he continue to wait? If there had been some sort of a cock-up, he could be left waiting for the rest of the day. They'd got Ralph's address, so they knew how to get hold of him . . .

He drove up the A20 to the Canterbury road, turned

on to this and continued northwards to Crampington Without. Without what? No one really knew. Immediately beyond Crampington Without a winding lane finally brought him to Rackington—a crossroads, a pub, a general store, and eight cottages—and a mile beyond, Parsonage Farm.

The parish church was over a mile and a quarter away and as far as was known Parsonage Farm had never belonged to the church, so that the origin of its name was as obscure as that of Crampington Without. It was a typical Kentish farmhouse—blue/red bricks, made locally, peg-tile roof, low, beamed ceilings, two central back-to-back inglenook fireplaces, and an atmosphere of quiet contentment. It was surrounded by a large garden and two acres of paddocks, while beyond these was the farm land which had been sold off years before.

Sterne drove in and parked the Mercedes to the side of the wooden double garage, then walked along the macadamed surface to the garden gate. Beyond, the path was made from bricks and it led round to the front door which faced the woods and not the road.

Angela stepped out of the house. 'Angus! . . . For heaven's sake, Angus!' She hugged him. 'What a wonderful surprise. Where on earth have you sprung from? I must phone Ralph and tell him you're here. It's only last night he was wondering how you were getting on . . . Are you hungry? Can I get you something?' She was a tall woman, thin from rigid dieting: her hair was a rich chestnut and naturally curly, her face was oval, regularly featured, and very photogenic. Before her marriage, she'd worked for a fashion magazine and several times she'd acted as a model. Had she wished, she could probably have made a very good career of modelling. It had been no surprise to those who knew her well that she had not so wished.

They went indoors and a Pekinese came out of the

sitting-room, having finally realized there was a visitor, and began to bark hysterically. Then it suddenly quietened and snuffled up to Sterne, feathered tail waving wildly. He bent down and stroked it.

'Lu always remembers you,' she said. 'It doesn't matter how long you've been away.'

'It's because I secretly give him tidbits.'

'Secretly!' She laughed. 'When Lu eats he makes so much noise the whole neighbourhood knows about it . . . But you've never told me—do you want a meal? I can very quickly knock something up.'

'Thanks, I had lunch on the way.'

'Then how about a coffee?'

'That would be great.'

'Come into the kitchen and tell me all your news while I make it.'

They drank the coffee in the sitting-room, dark because of the low, beamed ceiling, single small window, and the fact that it faced north. After a while, she looked at the jewelled wristwatch that Ralph had given her on their first wedding anniversary. 'I must be off to fetch one daughter from playschool and take her to a friend for tea.'

'How is Penny?'

'Penelope's very well, very noisy, and more stubborn than ever. The woman at the playschool who does afternoons says she's never met anyone so very determined.'

He must remember, he thought, not to call his niece Penny. Angela did not approve of the diminutive.

'Your bed's not made up, of course, but I'll see to that as soon as I get back. And if Mrs Lawson should ring whilst I'm out, will you tell her I'll bring the papers round as soon as I can. She's the new secretary of the WI. Quite a pleasant woman, but rather feather-brained. I have to spend half my time making certain she doesn't confuse everything . . . Oh, that reminds me—Madge may ring as well. I'll be able to do the meals-on-wheels on Thursday for her.'

'Still as busy as ever, then?'

'Of course.' Her father had taught her that rank carried duty. A major in the regular army who had failed to make lieutenant-colonel, he had been forcibly retired to civilian life which he had then organized with all the dedicated preciseness with which his service life had previously been run. It had probably never occurred to him that an occasional and timely relaxation from such certainty might have ensured the promotion which he had so coveted and which, on the face of things, he had been so well qualified to receive.

Angela drove away in her Datsun and Sterne, who'd accompanied her out of the house, brought from the Mercedes the suitcase and plastic bag. He left the bag on one of the occasional tables in the sitting-room, carried the suitcase up to the bedroom on the right-hand side of the small landing.

As soon as Angela and Ralph had moved into the house, she'd made a point of telling him that this was his bedroom, to be used whenever he wanted. A couple of his mother's primitive but attractive paintings hung on a wall, as did a framed prep-school photograph. He often looked at the four rows of boys and wondered how many of the one hundred and seventy-five were now pillars of society and how many were rebels, outcasts, or just plain wanderers? . . . From now on, he could no longer be a wanderer. He must conform. Angela would be glad. On the day he started work, she'd be able to refer to her brother-in-law without a hint of an apology in her voice.

Ralph Sterne was remarkably similar in appearance to his brother. The same light brown hair with a rolling curl at the front, the same light blue eyes, the same square jaw with a slight cleft. Even though there were nine years between them, each had at times been mistaken for the other: only when they were together was it obvious that Ralph's face was thicker, his colouring darker, his neck shorter, his body stockier.

'When I saw the car I thought it must be someone else important calling,' said Ralph, as he stood in the hall. 'Then it turns out to be only you.'

'For heaven's sake, Ralph, you might be a bit more welcoming after Angus has been away for so long.'

Ralph looked briefly at his wife, then grinned at his brother. Even after six years of marriage, Angela had never learned to understand their companionable joshing of each other. 'Well, how are things? And what's brought you back? The last time you wrote, you said you were remaining in Spain for at least the next three months.'

'I was dealt three kings and they never lose. Only this time they did.'

'You're saying you lost everything on a poker hand?'

'That's right.'

Angela was shocked. Even Ralph was surprised. Drawn into premature responsibility by the tragic death of his parents, he had learned to regard money as something one treated with great respect. Had he gambled—which he did not—he could no more have wagered a very large sum on one hand of cards than swindle one of his clients. 'If you're that broke, how come you arrive here in a Mercedes?'

'Simple—it's not mine. I was asked if I'd like to drive it back to the UK and as it offered a free trip here I jumped at the chance.'

'It's a nice-looking car,' said Angela, who was trying hard not to think that Angus had surely once again proved himself to have a weak character.

Ralph, who could guess how his wife's mind was working, hurriedly changed the conversation. 'What on earth are we doing standing here in the hall, when it's drinking time? Let's move into the sitting-room . . . Angy, what are you going to have to celebrate Angus's return?'

'Just my usual small sherry.'

'What's yours, Angus?'

'A large Scotch on the rocks.'

Ralph took one step, then came to a stop. 'I've just realized there's no sound of destruction going on in the house. So where's Penelope?'

'She's having tea with Brenda,' replied Angela.

'Sooner her than me. Even at her early age, Brenda gives every indication of growing up like her mother.'

'I've told you before, that's not being fair to Joyce.'

'Who's trying to be fair?' He went into the sitting-room and across to the small passageway which ran behind the massive central back-to-back fireplaces and chimneys—around which the house had been built—and opened the cocktail cabinet he kept there.

Angela had one glass of medium sweet sherry and then said she must go and fetch Penelope or Joyce would begin to worry. After she'd left, Ralph refilled Sterne's and his own glass and it was not by chance that his drink was stronger than before. Angela did not approve of drinking except as a social convention and Ralph had long since got into the habit of serving weak drinks when she was around even though she usually could have little idea of how much alcohol he'd given himself.

Twenty minutes later, Angela returned with her daughter. Penelope, not yet old enough to have learned restraint, threw herself on to Angus's lap and demanded her present, ignoring her mother's admonition that a well-brought-up girl did not ask for presents. She was given the doll and, grinning with a delight too great for words, switched it on. It walked with jerky strides and said 'Mama' in an irritatingly husky, corncrake voice. Lu immediately saw it as a potential rival and circled it, yapping wildly.

'That's enough for the moment,' Angela said, after a couple of minutes of near-bedlam.

'But Mummy . . .'

'It's upsetting Lu.'

'Then put beastly Lu in the kitchen.'

'You don't supplant an old friend with a new one.'

'What's supplant mean?'

'Just switch the doll off,' said Angela, who found any loud noise physically painful.

Penelope switched off the doll and very carefully carried it over to the box and laid it down in its polystyrene bed. Then she stood in front of Angus and asked if he'd brought her anything else.

Sterne, cutting off a fresh homily from Angela on the behaviour of young ladies, said no, he hadn't, because he'd thought she might prefer to go for a trip to Canterbury to choose something herself. She snuggled up to him by way of answer. He knew a sudden ambivalence: a warm happiness at being with the family and a quick annoyance that this should mean so much to him.

CHAPTER 7

The phone rang at a quarter past ten on Saturday morning and Ralph took the call in the hall. When he replaced the receiver, he said: 'That's odd.'

'What's odd?' asked Angela.

He ducked under the lintel—the house had been built when few men were taller than five foot nine—to enter the kitchen and crossed to the working surface where she was stirring a mixture in a bowl.'That looks good.'

'It should be. Apart from anything else, there's a pint of cream in there.'

'What's that going to do to our cholesterol count: put it in the stratosphere?'

'But I thought you'd like a special meal since Angus is back.'

'Can't think of anything nicer,' he replied, then kissed her on the back of her neck. He briefly wondered why she nearly always took life so seriously? 'So what's this exotic concoction called?'

'Angel's kiss. It's a recipe which comes from San Francisco.'

'Really? I thought all the angels had left there and only the fairies remained . . . What's in it besides cream?'

'Bananas, ground almonds, avocado pear, and a touch of ginger . . . Who was the phone call from?'

He reached out to the bowl, right forefinger extended.

'No you don't,' she said, raising the wooden spoon.

'Yes I do.' He scooped his forefinger into the mixture and then licked it. 'Delicious!'

'Just you try to steal any more . . . Now, will you please tell me who the phone call was from?'

'Jock McCall.'

'Who's he?'

'You know—the chap who works for Marston and Hall.

'That common little man who never shaves properly?'

He answered easily. 'He has a skin complaint which often prevents him shaving all of his face.'

'But presumably it wouldn't stop him using a pair of scissors if he wanted to?'

He didn't argue. His work had taught him that human nature cut across all social boundaries; her father had taught her that human nature was irrevocably bounded by them. 'Anyway, he's friendly with one of the inspectors in the local police force who told him in casual conversation that a watch is being kept from May House on orders from county HQ.'

'May House up the road?'

'Apparently.'

'What on earth could the police be watching for from there?'

'You tell me . . . That's why I said it was so odd.'

'He must have got things all mixed up.'

He was inclined to agree with her even though Jock McCall was a man who seldom made a mistake.

'May House?' said Sterne. 'But didn't I see a 'For Sale' board on the top road?'

Across the dining-room table, Ralph nodded. 'Been up for sale for over a year now. They're asking forty-five thousand and won't come down a penny, even though two of the outside walls are cracked, so it's small wonder no one's bought it.'

'Angus, would you like a little more?' asked Angela.

'I would,' said Penelope.

'Young lady, it's very rich and you've had enough.'

'No, I haven't, 'cause I'm still roomy.'

Sterne chuckled. 'Then you'd better fill up the spare room.'

Angela was about to complain that Angus was countenancing gluttony, when she checked the words. If she admonished him, she'd probably upset Ralph who was always hoping they'd get on better together. But much as she liked Angus as a person, she could not prevent herself despising him for a drifter. She gave Penelope half a spoonful more of Angel's Kiss, then divided what remained in the bowl between Ralph and Angus.

'What d'you think's meant by keeping watch on May House?' asked Sterne. 'If the house is empty, it can't be on anyone in it. And surely they can't be using the place to watch someone on the other side of the lane?'

Ralph chuckled. 'Old Mrs Piers would be horrified at the thought.'

Sterne ate a spoonful of the sweet. 'The orders came

down from county HQ?'

'That's what Jock said.'

'Wouldn't that suggest something pretty serious?'

'Almost certainly, yes . . . I wonder if there's a suggestion of corruption in the local division? But how in hell would a watch on May House help anyone investigate that?'

When Ralph had casually referred to what he'd heard earlier, Sterne's first, panicky thought had been that the police were watching the Mercedes. Second thoughts had momentarily reassured him. Even if the police believed the Mercedes might have been brought into the country on false papers, they'd never have set up an elaborate, time-consuming, expensive watch on it: they'd have come and demanded to see the papers . . . Then fresh doubts began to worry him. Could this watch have anything to do with the fact that his dealings with the Mercedes had not turned out as he'd expected? Evans had told him he must make the journey as quickly as possible and the woman in Lençon had given him a tight schedule to keep, yet no one had contacted him at the motel in Newingreen or here, at Parsonage Farm . . .

'Is something wrong?' Ralph asked.

He shook his head and spoke as casually as he could. 'Just wondering what it can all add up to?'

'Probably nothing. But if it does, we'll learn in good time. There's no such thing as a secret out here in the country.'

Soon afterwards, they cleared the table and packed the dirty plates and cutlery in the washing-up machine. That finished, Ralph and Sterne went through to the sitting-room while Angela remained in the kitchen to make coffee. Lu stayed with her, hoping against hope for some tidbits, and Penelope, for once obedient, went up to her bedroom to lie down on her bed and rest.

Three-quarters of an hour later, Ralph left to go into

the library to do some work which had to be completed before Monday, and Sterne said he'd like to go for a walk, to counter the effects of the delicious lunch.

Ten minutes later he drew level with an old wooden bungalow, to which had been added a brick-built extension, and an elderly woman who had been weeding a flowerbed, came to her feet and said: 'It's Mr Angus, ain't it?'

He went into the garden and spoke to Mrs Piers, eighty-one years old and sufficiently independent in manner to be considered either a character or rude. Certainly she was eccentric in that she still showed an old-fashioned degree of respect towards those she considered deserved it. He was always Mr Angus, his brother was always Mr Ralph.

They talked about her rheumatism, her nephews and nieces, and the local vicar who was so mistaken as to think that he'd communicate more easily with his parishioners if he sometimes wore an open-neck shirt . . .

There was a pause and Sterne said casually: 'I hear someone's moved into May House?'

'Who says? The board's still showin'. Saw it meself this mornin' when I was going to the village.' She still walked to the village and back at least three times a week and found nothing extraordinary in this.

'In that case, I expect the story's wrong.'

'Wouldn't be the first time.' She chuckled, had hastily to adjust her lower plate.

'You've not seen anyone over there?'

'Can't see nothing now but the roof, what with the hedge being allowed to grow so high. Mind you, there 'as been cars driving up of a night. But that'll be the youngsters. Always at it, they are, these days.' Was there a trace of regret for past opportunities denied in her voice.

'At what sort of times do the cars go up?'

'All times. I don't sleep so well, so I 'ear 'em.'

'Would you say, very late?'

'Two, three, four—time don't mean nothing when they're young. Don't mean nothing to you, I'll be bound. 'Specially with them foreign girls. Seen a lot of 'em, I'll lay.'

She was presuming that it was he who had done the laying. He hinted at many wild nights and she chuckled, and when he left her eyes were bright with memories.

He returned to the lane and continued on past a row of brick-built cottages to the Rackington/Bybrook road. Two hundred yards along to the right, set in an overgrown thorn hedge, was a gateway. The straining-post had rotted at ground level and the wooden five-bar gate, top rail broken, was resting on the ground. Beyond the gateway was an estate agent's board, giving brief and optimistic details of the very desirable Edwardian family house.

From the gateway, only the slate roof of the house was visible. He walked along the drive which remained almost level for a while, then dropped quite sharply. The house came into view, segment by segment: square, box-shaped, with bow windows, it looked like some surburban refugee.

There was no sign of life. All the windows were closed and the garden was a riot of grass and weeds. The detached brick garage, with wooden doors, was shut. He remembered that Mrs Piers had said that she'd heard cars driving down here . . . The gravel surface in front of the garage was disturbed, as it would be if the garage had recently been used. He examined the doors. There was provision for securing them with an external padlock, but none was evident. He turned the handle and pulled and the door opened. Inside was a battered yellow Metro.

He closed the garage door and stared at the house once more, then beyond it. Because the land sloped all the way to the bottom lane, the drive and garage of Parsonage Farm were clearly visible, as was the Mercedes . . .

The front door of the house opened and a man stepped out under the small porch over which grew a pink Montana clematis. He was dressed in a lightweight sweater and jeans and there was a suggestion of hard watchfulness to his chunky face. 'Wanting something, mate?'

'The house is for sale so I'm looking around.'

'Have you been on to the agents?'

'No.'

'Then you'd better do that. It's viewing by appointment only.'

'The board didn't say so.'

The man shrugged his shoulders.

Sterne saw that a second man was studying him from one of the upstairs windows. 'It looks as if you've moved in—so is the place still for sale?'

'If you want to know anything, speak to the agents.'

'I suppose they do know you're here?'

'That's right.'

Sterne turned and walked back up the drive. An icy fear grew with every pace. Jock McCall had been only too right, the police were keeping watch from the house. And it was almost impossible to guess what they were interested in if it wasn't the Mercedes parked outside the garage at Parsonage Farm.

CHAPTER 8

Angela was a person of routine so tea was served—barring earthquakes—at 5.45.

They had almost finished—Ralph had just been poured his second cup—when they heard a car drive in.

'I do hope that's not Fiona, come to collect the jam. She'll never leave,' said Angela, with the petulance of a woman whose days were planned and who disliked any unscheduled interruption.

Ralph ducked under the central, roughly shaped beam and crossed to the window. 'Does she have a red car?'

'Hers is silver and Hugh's is a hideous green.'

'Then it's not Fiona . . . It's a couple of men—don't recognize them from here.'

'Perhaps they've come to eat,' said Penelope.

Angela's expression suggested that if that were the case, their visitors would be disappointed.

Ralph went into the hall as the two men entered the garden and as they came up to the front door he recognized the younger. He opened the door and Lu, who'd followed him, began to yap. 'Shut up,' he said. Since that had no effect, and Angela could not see him, he gently used the toe of his shoe to add emphasis to his command and with sulky ill-grace Lu became quiet. He opened the door. ' 'Evening, Meacher,' he said to the detective-sergeant, whom he'd met many times in the local magistrates' courts.

''Evening, Mr Sterne. Sorry to bother you at this time of the evening, but we'd like a bit of a chat.'

'Come on in.' He stepped to one side and the two men entered.

'This is Detective-Superintendent Young.'

Ralph shook hands with the heavily built man, in his middle fifties, who had a round, full face with noticeably protruding ears. His manner was genial and open and with his country suit and well-coloured face he could have been a prosperous farmer. Yet, Ralph noted, there was a sense of reserve which suggested that behind his bluff friendliness there lay a shrewdness and, perhaps, even a hardness. He was not a man Ralph knew. 'Are you from county HQ?'

'That's right,' replied Young, in his deep, baritone

voice. 'So I grab every possible chance to come down to this part of the world. It's still what I call real country and that's getting rare.'

'And will get rarer with commuters flooding further and further out.' For years Ralph had fought against the urbanization of the countryside, careless of the fact that it was a long-since lost cause. 'So what's brought you here? Some sort of problem?'

'In a way, but it really concerns your brother. Is he here now?'

'Angus? Yes, he's here. What's the trouble with him?'

'We'd like a word with him.'

'A word about what?'

Young did not answer.

Ralph said: 'We might as well use the dining-room: any minute now, television will be switched on for our daughter.'

'*Billy the Brune*?' asked Young.

'How's that?'

'I have an idea that's the cartoon which comes on this afternoon for the children. I always watch it if I have the chance.'

There was something faintly ludicrous in the thought of a man like Young watching so infantile a cartoon.

Ralph led the way through the hall and kitchen into the dining-room. 'The chairs are more comfortable than they look,' he said, indicating the heavy wooden priory chairs with solid backs and crossed legs secured with pegs. 'Would you like something to drink?'

'Not for us, thanks,' answered Young.

Meacher looked sour.

Ralph left the dining-room by way of the short passage and eased his way past the cocktail cabinet to enter the sitting-room. Angela was packing the tray. 'Your coffee's there, on the table.'

'I won't bother with it.'

'But you . . .'

'The two men are policemen and they've come to have a word with Angus.' He was watching his brother's face as he spoke and the expression he saw there frightened him—he'd seen guilt too often not to recognize it.

'Policemen to see Angus?' said Angela, as she moved the plates to make room for the milk jug. 'What on earth about?'

'They haven't said.'

'It's too late for that sort of thing. Tell them to come back some other time.'

He spoke quietly. 'It's probably better if we get it over and done with now.'

Penelope said loudly: 'I want the television.'

'What . . . what are they after?' asked Sterne, all too conscious that his voice was higher pitched than usual.

'I've just said, I don't know yet.'

Sterne struggled to reassure himself. From what Evans had said, the running of cars from Spain was a regular traffic, so surely the organizers had had considerable practice in supplying authentic-seeming papers? In that case, provided he could put up a casually detailed story, as an innocent would, he'd have every chance of bluffing his way out of trouble . . .

'Are you coming?' asked Ralph.

Angela looked up, not missing the suggestion of tension. 'Darling, what is the matter?'

'I just want to get it over and done with, that's all.'

As the two men left, Penelope demanded to know why she wasn't being allowed to watch the television.

Sterne's first judgement was that the older man was easy-going and the younger one was much harder and therefore the one to be wary of.

'Mr Angus Sterne? I'm Detective-Superintendent Young and my companion is Detective-Sergeant Meacher.' He did not come forward to shake hands.

Instead he sat and with that one action he took charge of the interview. He waited until Ralph and Sterne were seated, on the opposite side of the table, then said to Sterne: 'Is that Mercedes in the drive yours?'

'Yes.'

'It does belong to you?'

'Yes.' Sterne was conscious of the quick look Ralph gave him—he remembered his saying that the car wasn't his, he'd been asked to drive it back . . .

'How long have you owned it?'

'Not very long.'

'Where did you buy it?'

'In Cagnes.'

'Who did you buy it from?'

'A man called Pritchard.'

'Is he a friend?'

'Rather an acquaintance.'

'Why was he selling it?'

'He'd decided to live in France and reckoned it would obviously be much more suitable to run a left-hand drive car.'

'In what currency did you pay him?'

'Francs. I offered him dollars but he chose francs because he reckoned the dollar was about to slide a bit.'

'I imagine you've some kind of receipt to detail this sale?'

'In the glove locker, along with all the other relevant papers.'

Young turned to the detective-sergeant. 'Let's have the report.'

Meacher produced a folded sheet of paper and handed this over. Young put on a pair of spectacles and read. He looked up. 'You returned to this country with the car last Sunday.'

'Monday,' corrected Ralph, with the sharpness of someone who knew the importance of making certain that even the least relevant detail was correct.

Young looked at Ralph over the tops of his spectacles. 'Are you sure? My information is that it was Sunday, the fourteenth.' He turned to Sterne. 'Which is correct?'

'Sunday,' muttered Sterne.

Young seemed unsurprised that Ralph should have made a mistake over the date of his brother's return. 'You arrived on the seven-thirty cross Channel ferry to find that a . . . What the hell's the name of it?'

'A blanket search,' said Meacher.

'Yes, of course. I knew it was something to do with a bed, but could only think of counterpane . . . You arrived at Dover to find a blanket search was in progress. Your car and luggage were thoroughly checked. Was anything of an illegal nature found?'

'No,' replied Stone, his confidence increasing because it seemed that Young was going to do all the questioning.

Young dropped the paper on to the table, removed the glasses but held them in his right hand. He studied Sterne. 'During the search of your luggage you were observed to be in a nervous state. Why was that?'

'I wasn't.'

'The observation is quite definite.'

Ralph said sharply: 'That can be no more than an assumption.'

'Customs officers are trained to interpret the behaviour patterns of the people with whom they come in contact.'

'Nevertheless, without proof, they can only ever come to assumptions.'

'Perhaps we're in danger of becoming tangled-up with the problems of semantics . . . I'll try to put things in a different way.' He turned to Sterne. 'Would you like to suggest why the Customs officer who searched your luggage should have become convinced that you had something to fear from that search?'

Ralph spoke immediately. 'My brother can hardly

illuminate the course of another man's thoughts.'

'That isn't exactly what I meant.'

'Perhaps. But it's that that you asked him to do.'

Young shrugged his shoulders. 'I've always liked to handle a case in the most discreet manner because in the long run that's best for both sides. So right now I'm more concerned with discovering the truth than I am in making certain every question I put is exact, unambiguous, and admissible in a court of law . . . Perhaps it would be easier if I spoke to your brother on his own.'

'You may be prepared to ignore the rules governing the questioning of witnesses; I am not prepared to let you.'

'To ignore the rules . . . I don't think I've been doing that.' He turned back to Sterne. 'Do you have any objection to your car being searched again by us?'

Sterne had been expecting, and dreading, more questions concerning the purchase of the car so this question came as a relief. 'No, of course not.'

'May we take it with us when we leave?'

Ralph said: 'You have an authorization for this action?'

'We have your brother's agreement.'

'He did not understand the full implication of what he was agreeing to.'

Young, in the same easy tone, as if his patience were infinite, said to Sterne: 'Are we likely to find anything of an illegal nature in or about your car?'

'No.'

'So you have no reason to fear our search?'

'None.'

Ralph said: 'What do you expect to find?'

'I can't answer that.' He held up his left hand. 'Not because I'm refusing to, but because I just don't know.'

'You're obviously convinced that there is something to find.'

'The possibility is there, yes.'

'Merely because a Customs officer imagined my

brother was nervous?'

'You may put it like that.'

'I can, and I'd be talking nonsense if I did. If the Customs had really thought that, they'd have taken the car apart then and there . . . Have you been keeping watch on this house and grounds from May House?'

'I'm sure you can answer your own question.'

'Why are you sure?'

'Your brother will have told you the answer.'

'He's told me nothing. How could he?'

Young looked surprised. He put his spectacles back in their case.

'How could he have told me?' demanded Ralph.

'This afternoon, he walked up to May House and spoke to one of my men. I presumed, from the report of this meeting, that your brother had correctly judged what was going on.' He stood. 'May we have the keys to the Mercedes?'

Sterne handed them over to Meacher.

'We'll return the car to you just as soon as we're satisfied it's clean . . . Thank you both for your co-operation.' The words could have been ironic, but Young's expression remained bland.

Five minutes later, after the detectives had driven off in the two cars, Ralph said: 'What the hell's going on?'

'Nothing's going on,' replied Sterne.

'Don't be so goddamn stupid. Christ! it's like when you were a kid and you'd go on and on denying something when it was obvious . . . Why didn't you tell me you'd been up to May House and found the police were keeping watch?'

Sterne shrugged his shoulders.

'You told us you came over on the Monday, now I learn it was on the Sunday. You told us the car isn't yours, you tell the police it is. Why all the lies? How could you afford a car like that when you'd gambled everything away? The police don't keep watch on someone just because they think he's smuggled in a couple of bottles of whisky extra. What the hell have you been up to?'

'I need a drink,' said Sterne thickly. He went into the small passage, opened the cocktail cabinet and poured out two whiskies. He returned and handed one glass to Ralph.

'Well?'

'I drove the car back from Spain, not France.'

'Where's the significance in that?'

He explained.

Ralph said, in tones of amazement: 'Didn't you realize what you were doing?'

'Of course I did.'

'You *knew* you were breaking the law?'

'Come off it. All I was doing was helping avoid a ridiculous tax that should never have been imposed in the first case.'

'But the law's the law, whatever you think of it.'

'Not when the law's a bloody ass.'

As he drank, Ralph wondered, with something akin to hurt, how his brother could regard the law with such contempt.

Ralph climbed into the right-hand side of the king-size bed, placed a pillow for support, then leaned back and began to read a paperback.

'Ralph.'

He looked up. Angela had fixed her frock on a hanger and she was now putting the hanger in the cupboard which had been fashioned out of the space between the rising chimneys and the outside wall.

'What did those policemen want?'

'I told you.'

She closed the cupboard door, returned to her side of the bed, unzipped a flowered case to bring out a nightdress. 'You're worried stiff about something. I'm sure you've not told me everything that happened.'

He wondered why it was that his emotions were always an open book to her, but hers were mostly an enciphered mystery to him.

She finished undressing with economical ease, slipped the nightdress over her head. She walked up to the side of the bed, stared at him, and said: 'What really happened?'

'Angus . . . He may be in a spot of trouble.'

'Police trouble?'

Her voice had risen and her expression had become strained; she reacted immediately, some would add excessively, to anything which threatened her world of husband and child. Speaking easily, trying to make light of what he was saying, he told her.

'Does that mean he'll be taken to court?'

'If the police should uncover proof of the attempted evasion of taxes, yes.'

'And then it'll be in all the papers?'

'It may be, it may not be. If things should go that far, it would all depend on how much novelty news value the editor reckons the story has.'

'Novelty?' she said bitterly. 'Everyone will know your brother's a crook.'

'There's every chance it won't come to that. If the car documents are sufficiently good, the police may suspect yet not be able to prove the facts sufficiently to take the case to court.'

'Why did he do it?'

'God knows.'

'After all you've done for him, he repays you by dragging you into trouble. He doesn't give a damn about hurting us.'

She sounded completely selfish, but he knew that, in fact, it was not selfishness which made her speak like that: it was fear. Not only fear that her family might directly suffer, but also fear that the badge of respectability might be torn from them. He reached out and put his hand lightly on her arm. 'Don't get too upset, love. As I said, maybe the police won't be able to prove anything. And in any case, it's not a serious matter.' He didn't believe that and she knew that he didn't. For him, the slightest criminal offence was a serious one. A free and democratic society, gift of the ancient Greeks, depended in the final analysis not so much on the moral standards of its people or the quality of its leaders, but on just laws being rigorously observed. So that each time any law, however minor, was broken, democracy was put at risk.

She climbed into bed and they both read. Fifteen minutes later he closed his paperback, put it down on the small bedside table, switched off the light, and settled for sleep.

'Ralph, just now you told me it wasn't a serious matter?'

'That's right.'

'Yet this afternoon you said that the police would only maintain a serious watch on anywhere if something very serious were wrong.'

CHAPTER 9

On Sunday morning Angela went to church, as she did every alternate week: services were held every other Sunday in Rackington parish church. She was always slightly hurt that she could so seldom persuade Ralph to accompany her: in the country, the conduct of the few were still of interest and concern to the many.

At eleven forty-five, Ralph left Parsonage Farm to drive Penelope to friends who had a daughter of the same age with whom Penelope would, provided open warfare did not break out, have lunch and spend the afternoon.

Sterne, who'd offered to mow the lawn—Ralph was far from a keen gardener—wheeled the mower out from the shed next to the garage and then spent the next quarter of an hour coaxing it into life. He'd cut no more than a dozen swaths when a car drove in. He looked up, surprised that Ralph had returned so soon and saw over the hedge not the Jaguar but a red Metro. As he watched, Young and Meacher climbed out of the car and once again he knew an icy fear.

'I was hoping we'd find you in,' said Young. 'Is your brother here as well?'

'Not at the moment.'

Young's expression didn't alter, but Meacher looked as if he'd just heard some good news.

Sterne spoke challengingly. 'I thought you promised to bring my car back this morning?'

'True enough,' replied Young. 'But something's cropped up and we've come to talk about it.'

In the sitting-room, Young settled in one of the armchairs with the air of a man who might be staying quite a while. 'How did you hear about the Mercedes being for sale?'

Sterne remembered a drunken Irishman, in a bar in San Remo, who'd insisted on advising everyone on how to avoid being arrested. 'Never tell the bastards anything for certain: then they can't prove you're a bleeding liar.' 'I don't remember now.'

'Where were you?'

'In France.'

'France is quite a big country.'

He noticed that Meacher was writing in a notebook. 'I was on the move—Menton, Nice, Cannes, St Tropez—and it's difficult to pin anything like that down.'

'The owner lived where?'

'Cagnes. It's in the car papers somewhere.'

'What did you pay for it?'

'A hundred and ten thousand francs: that's also in them.'

'You had quite a lot of money?'

'I had a win at the casino.'

'How much?'

'Near a hundred and fifty thousand francs.'

'That's quite an impressive win.'

'I was impressed.'

'The man who broke the bank at Monte Carlo.'

'It wasn't Monte Carlo and in these days it would take very much more than that to break any bank. I've seen one man put on two hundred thousand francs every turn of the wheel.'

'You heard of this car, you had the money to buy it, and you bought it. Why?'

'Isn't that obvious?'

'If it was, I wouldn't ask the question.'

'I'd decided to return home and I'd got to make the journey somehow and here was the chance to make it a profitable journey.'

'Why profitable?'

'The car's worth more here than I paid for it there because it's right-hand drive.'

'Then you're not thinking of keeping it?'

'I'm not in that sort of tax bracket.'

'What route did you take through France on your way back to this country?'

'A slow one, roughly up through the Tarn, Dordogne, and châteaux district.'

'My geography's weak, but that wasn't a very direct route, was it?'

'It wasn't meant to be.'

'Then you weren't in a hurry?'

'I had a little time to spare.'

'Would you detail your route more exactly?'

'Why?'

Before Young could reply, they heard a car stop and the slam of a door. Sterne stood and through the window saw Ralph walking quickly up the drive. 'It's my brother.'

'Wouldn't be complete without him,' said Meacher, to Young's evident annoyance.

When Ralph entered the room, he was breathing heavily. Young stood and Meacher, reluctantly, did the same. 'What are you doing here on a Sunday?' Ralph asked, his voice clipped.

'We've come to ask your brother a few more questions.'

'Have you returned the Mercedes?'

'Not yet.'

'Have you found anything?'

Young did not answer. He sat once more.

'If you've not found anything, there's no point to your questioning my brother again.'

'He can help me with my inquiries.'

'What inquiries—if there was nothing?'

Young spoke to Ralph, but he studied Sterne. 'Hidden in one of the side members of the Mercedes was a metal container.'

'That's impossible,' said Sterne immediately.

'Why?'

'Because . . .' He stopped.

'What was in the container?' demanded Ralph.

'Traces.'

'Of what?'

'The container has been sent to the forensic laboratory and until they've identified the traces I won't be able to answer you.'

'What did they look like?'

'They were a fine white powder.'

Ralph's expression was shocked and his voice had lost much of its belligerence. 'Even if you don't know for certain, you must have some idea what that powder is?'

'Possibly. But I am not prepared to put a name to it now.'

'There couldn't have been any container,' said Sterne.

'Why not?'

'I had a mechanic check the car.'

'Where?'

'In . . . in Cagnes.'

Ralph said quickly: 'If the traces turn out to be innocuous, no offence has been committed. Therefore at this stage you are not in a position to say whether or not you're investigating a criminal matter.'

'So?'

'You have no right to question my brother on the assumption that the contents are not innocuous.'

'You're the lawyer, not me,' said Young mildly, 'but I'd have said that my questions were aimed merely at finding out if your brother knew about the container.'

'He's answered you. He didn't.'

Young spoke to Sterne. 'You are quite certain you knew nothing about it?'

'Of course I am.'

Young came to his feet with an easy speed which was unusual for a man of his age and size. His expression remained pleasant, but his voice had hardened. 'We'll leave now. No doubt we'll meet again.'

As the Metro drove on to the road, Ralph turned round from the window of the sitting-room. 'You understand, don't you?' he said thickly.

'He thinks it's hard drugs,' replied Sterne.

'He knows it is. But until he has the laboratory proof, he can't do anything. Christ! Dope-running.'

'You think I've been running drugs?'

'There's no argument. The container was on the Mercedes when it came into this country so you've been running them . . . Obviously, there was a tip-off. The Customs at Dover didn't know which car, so they checked the lot and found the container on yours, but said nothing to you. The police kept watch on you to try and discover who your contacts were who'd take delivery. But you blew their cover . . .'

'You're talking as if I knew all the time. D'you think I'd knowingly run drugs into this country?'

'No.'

'From the way you've just been talking, you do.'

'I'm trying to make you understand the way things are.'

'I can prove I didn't know about the container.'

'How?'

'I got a mechanic in Cala Survas to check the car was clean.'

'Why?'

'For God's sake, I've just told you.'

'And you've also told me, through inference, that you knew then that you were being offered too much for just driving a car back with false papers.'

'It wasn't that certain. I mean, the money was more, but not crazy. I just wanted to be certain.'

'Or did you want something to fall back on if you were caught?'

'Goddamn it, whose side are you on?'

'Yours,' said Ralph, with bitter weariness.

'You could have fooled me.'

'I have to try and visualize things as the police see them if I'm to know what to do that'll help you the most.'

Sterne jammed his hands in his trouser pockets. 'I didn't know about the container.'

'Circumstances say you did.'

'Then the circumstances are bloody liars.'

'You're forgetting all about the car, aren't you?'

'I thought that's what we'd just been talking about.'

'It's worth what—fifteen thousand, maybe more. And it's in your name.'

'They were supposed to collect it at Newingreen.'

'There's only your word for that.'

'The police can't claim the car was part of the price.'

'In the circumstances, they're hardly likely to say anything else.'

'But . . .'

'Angus, don't you still understand the picture? They're tipped off that someone's running drugs by car. You arrive in a Mercedes and you're in a nervous sweat. They find the container, but don't do anything immediately because you're the runner and they want the principals. In the end, you blow their cover and so they have to move. Then they discover that the heroin's already gone, right from under their noses. They're bitter and angry so now they're determined to land you. And they know that you brought the stuff in and you've a nearly new Mercedes in payment for the run.'

'It's not like that at all,' said Sterne desperately.

'But that's how it looks to the police.'

'How do I prove they're wrong?'

Ralph walked over to the large inglenook fireplace and stood with his back to it. When he spoke, his voice was tired. 'You've only one course left open. You'll have to admit that you were trying to carry out a tax swindle.'

At four, Angela said it was time to fetch Penelope and Sterne offered to go if he could borrow a car. Later, when her Datsun had driven out, Angela, sitting very upright in one of the armchairs, said: 'What's happened?'

'Nothing in particular,' Ralph replied.

'Please don't be so stupid. I can always tell when you're worried and ever since I got back you've been terribly worried.'

Just for a moment, Ralph hated his brother for bringing such trouble to their home.

'Well—are you going to tell me?'

He cleared his throat. 'While you were out, the police

called again. When they searched the Mercedes, they found . . . a container in which were traces of a white powder. The container's been sent off for tests and until he gets the results the detective-superintendent won't say what he reckons the traces are. But there's no doubt. Heroin.'

'Oh my God! . . . What are you going to do?'

'I've told Angus he's got to admit to the police that he was trying a tax swindle.'

'How can that help?'

'It explains why he was nervous at the Customs search and why it's not true that he was being paid too much merely for driving the Mercedes into this country. It'll help him to show he'd no idea drugs had been planted on the car or that the real mission of his journey was drug-smuggling.'

'You're saying he's got to prove all that?'

'Yes. But once he tells them the full truth, they'll realize what happened.' He was trying to convince not only her but himself.

CHAPTER 10

Divisional HQ was in south Fording Cross, six miles from Rackington. Once a pleasant, in parts historical, market town, the electrification of the main railway line had brought Fording Cross within commuting distance of London so that before long its population had doubled. Left to cope with this increase by the well-tried precedent of trial and error, the town would almost certainly have managed to retain at least some of its character, but it had been held that only expert planning could or would solve the problems. Within fifteen years, careful and expert planning managed to turn the town into one more dreary example of municipal bad taste.

Divisional HQ was a ten-storey concrete and glass block, just north of the railway. It had won an architectural competition. It was that sort of a building. It stood one road back from the parish church, a seventeenth-century picture of quiet harmony, and the contrast could not have been more marked. As one defeated and bitter conservationist had remarked, it was a wonder that the church had not been knocked down since it was so obviously a visual anomaly.

At the entrance gates, Ralph came to a stop. 'Don't elaborate. Whatever happens, don't elaborate. Just give them the plain facts.'

Ironically, Sterne thought, that was the same advice as the drunken Irishman in the bar in San Remo had given.

The ground floor of the building was a car park and a spiral ramp led from the entrance to the front room on the first floor. Long and narrow, the desk was at the far end. Ralph went across and spoke to the duty sergeant, who telephoned the office Detective-Superintendent Young was using while working from the building. After replacing the receiver, he said to Ralph that Mr Young would be with him as soon as possible.

It was ten minutes before a uniform PC came across to the table at which they were both sitting, leafing through some out-of-date magazines, and said: 'Mr Sterne? Would you come this way, please?'

They followed him along one passage and down another to an interview room. This was square, functional, painted in two shades of institutional brown, and it contained only a wooden table, four chairs, and a framed list of the rights of witnesses. There was one small window and this was set high up and barred.

Young entered, followed by a second man whom he introduced as DC Best. They sat at the table and Best opened a notebook and prepared to write.

'Well, how can I help you?' asked Young.

Ralph spoke with careful slowness. 'After you left my house yesterday, I talked over certain matters with my brother. In consequence of what he told me, I decided it would be best if he came here and made a statement to you.'

'Presumably, in connection with the Mercedes and the container we found in it?'

'Yes.'

Young turned to Sterne. 'Would you like to make that statement now? And I would add the customary advice that what you say will be taken down in writing and may be used in evidence.'

Sterne explained what had happened in Spain and France.

Young said: 'In whose name was the car when you left Spain?'

'Brian Ridgeway.'

'Do you have papers to confirm that?'

'They were taken from me when I was given the fresh ones in Lençon.'

'If you'd been stopped at the French border, how would you have explained the fact that the car wasn't yours?'

'I'd have said I'd been asked to drive it back to the UK by a friend.'

'Which would have been an equally satisfactory reason to give, had the same question been put to you on your arrival in England?'

Ralph said: 'That situation didn't arise. It would be better if we stick to the facts.'

Young smiled, with brief, ironic amusement. He said to Sterne: 'Were you at all surprised when the woman handed you a new set of papers in Lençon and you found that the car was now in your name?'

'Yes, I was: very.'

'Did you ask her why this was?'

'No. I just presumed it was better if it was in my name when I entered England, in case any questions were asked.'

'But you'd been quite happy to cross from Spain into France with the car registered in the name of Ridgeway?'

'I'd have been equally happy to continue on to this country. But if they wanted to do it another way, I wasn't going to argue.'

'Did it occur to you that with the car in your name you'd be in a position to sell it, if you wished?'

'I didn't wish.'

'Or you could just keep it.'

'I wasn't going to keep it either. I intended to hand it over to whoever came to collect it.'

'But no one came?'

'I expected someone to meet me at Newingreen.'

'What did you do on your arrival at the motel?'

'Had a meal, watched the television for a little, and then, because I was tired, went to bed.'

'No one came to your cabin at any time during the night?'

'No.'

'And in the morning, what did you do?'

'Had breakfast, waited around until lunch, and then drove to my brother's.'

'Are you surprised that no one's attempted to collect so valuable a car?'

'Yes.'

'Since the quicker they got their hands on it, the quicker they could sell it and realize the profit, you'd have expected them to have collected it at the first possible moment?'

Ralph interrupted. 'My brother's already answered that.'

'Has he?' said Young blandly. He asked Sterne: 'While you've been staying with your brother, you've heard nothing?'

'No.'

'You've not tried to get in touch with anyone to find out why they haven't collected the car?'

'I've no way of doing that.'

'You couldn't, for instance, have had a word with Evans in Cala Survas?'

It had never occurred to Sterne to do that: he realized how damaging such an admission might appear to be.

Young waited, then said: 'What's his address?'

'Seventeen, Calle Primo de Rivera.'

'We'll see if the Spanish police can have a talk with him . . . You say you were paid five hundred dollars for expenses and a hundred and fifty pounds more were to be paid on delivery?'

'Yes.'

Young scratched his strong, square chin with his thumb and forefinger. 'That seems to have covered everything for the moment.'

Ralph said: 'My brother had the car checked for any extraneous objects in Spain.'

'So he mentioned.'

'That shows he'd no intention of smuggling.'

'I suppose that's one interpretation of the facts.'

They returned to the Jaguar, in the municipal car park. 'Well?' said Sterne, as he settled in the front passenger seat. 'Did he believe me?'

'He'll check up on your story as far as possible.'

'That's not what I asked.'

'You must remember, policemen are professional cynics.'

'Likewise solicitors?'

CHAPTER 11

Sterne was outside in the garden of Parsonage Farm when the phone rang. Through one of the hall windows he saw Angela walk up to the corner cupboard and pick up the receiver. She continued talking and it became obvious the call was not for him. He knew fresh despair. It was now nearly a fortnight since he'd landed at Dover and still no one had contacted him about the Mercedes: until someone did his story must, at best, look weak: at worst, a feeble lie.

He'd known nothing about the container, yet how was he to prove his innocence? How did one prove that one hadn't known something when all the surrounding circumstances suggested that one must have done? How could he convince the detective-superintendent that he'd told the truth when all the time no one tried to claim the Mercedes? . . . Until now, he'd always assumed that truth was objective and certain. Now, he was learning differently. Truth was how the other person subjectively viewed the facts.

He crossed the lawn to the old apple tree which each year produced a crop of rosy-streaked Bramleys, some as large as grapefruit, and stared out at the woods which lay beyond a dip in the land. Unless he could find a way to prove the truth, the woods, the garden, the apple tree, the mellowed farmhouse, might all retreat until they became no more than a bitter, painful memory, haunting him in prison . . .

He heard Angela approach and turned.

'That was the Watsons on the phone. We're invited to a meal on Tuesday evening.'

'Fine. I'll babysit.'

'All three of us. When I told them you were staying, they immediately said you were to go as well.'

'That's very kind, but it might be best if I remain behind.'

She bent down and began to search amongst the grass.

'Have you lost something?' he asked.

'I'm looking for a four-leaf clover because I found one around here last year. Perhaps if I could find another . . .' She tailed off into silence, embarrassed by her childish longing to find something magical which would immediately set the world right. She came upright and smoothed down her printed linen skirt.

'It looks like I'll need a whole armful of four-leaf clover,' he said bitterly.

She stared out at the woods and the sun underlined the strength of character in her face.

'I'm terribly sorry,' he said quietly.

'For what?'

'For involving you in a situation where I'm likely to cause a stink.'

'Angus. Did you know about the heroin?'

'No.'

'You never began to wonder if it might be something like that?'

'Only at the very beginning, which is why I had the car searched. It never occurred to me to have the same thing done after Lençon. Christ! how can anyone think I'd willingly smuggle drugs? And could I have stayed with you if I had, knowing you could become implicated?'

She turned and stared intently at him. After a while she said: 'No, you could never have done a thing like that. You'd have stayed right away from us . . . Ralph's doing everything he can.'

'I know he is.'

'He'll find a way of helping you.'

'I'm sure he will.' Only he wasn't.

*

Young telephoned on the following Monday morning, just as the rain began to fall to make a mockery of the weather forecast. Could Angus Sterne come to the station, please.

Ralph, who'd been about to leave to go to the office, stood in the hall and tried to keep the fresh fear from his face—when the police started asking someone to go to the station instead of their coming to his house it meant that in their eyes he'd made the final and irrevocable change from witness to suspect . . . He said to Sterne: 'Say we'll be there at ten.'

Sterne rang off.

'Maybe they've at last found out something,' said Angela.

'Who's found out?' asked Penelope.

'Don't listen in to other people's conversations.'

'You were listening in to Uncle Angus.'

'That's different.'

'Why?'

Angela abruptly changed the conversation. 'Why have you got up from the table?'

' 'Cause I've eaten enough.'

'Then kindly go and clear your place.'

Reluctantly, Penelope left the kitchen to go into the dining-room, closely followed by Lu, sniffing energetically and hoping for a tidbit despite the house rules.

'Perhaps they've traced whoever it was who was meant to collect the car?' suggested Angela.

'It could be,' replied Ralph. She had a sharp intelligence, yet experience had taught him that when faced with something unpleasant she often seemed to bury her head in the sands of ignorance.

'Keep looking for that four-leaf clover,' said Sterne.

'I'll find one,' she said, with hard determination.

*

They spoke to Young in the same interview room as before: this time, Meacher was the second detective.

Young had carried in a folder and he opened this and brought out a sheet of paper. 'Mr Sterne, do you know how much tax should have been paid on the Mercedes on its re-importation into this country?'

'No, I don't.'

'Would you like to hazard a figure?'

'If he's no idea,' objected Ralph, 'he's not in a position to make any estimate whatsoever.'

Young read what was written on the sheet of paper, looked up. 'I have been given the figure of two hundred and thirty pounds. You said previously you were paid five hundred dollars in expenses. Taking the exchange rate in today's paper, that's three hundred and thirty pounds. I've spoken to a colleague who's very recently driven up from Barcelona and his estimate is that the one-way journey from Cala Survas in a Mercedes would cost about a hundred and eighty pounds, remembering that the motel room was paid for. Would you agree?'

'It's impossible to agree or disagree without a careful study of the facts,' said Ralph.

'For the moment, we'll assume the figure is about right. That means you received one hundred and fifty pounds over and above the expenses reasonably likely to be involved—or, to put it another way, a hundred and fifty more than one of the organizers would have needed if he'd been making the journey. On top of that, you'd been promised a hundred and fifty pounds on delivery. That makes a total of three hundred pounds or seventy pounds more than if the car had been declared as coming from Spain.'

'That figure has no direct relevance,' snapped Ralph. 'The car in England is worth considerably more than the car in Spain.'

'Of course. But I think you've missed my point which is that—whatever the relative values—to drive the car back and declare it, rather than paying your brother to smuggle it through, would have saved them money.'

'You have obviously only been able to reach that figure after considerable research. If you couldn't work it out without that, how was my brother to do so without the means to make any research?'

Young ignored the questions. 'Mr Sterne, didn't it strike you as a lot of money if the job was merely to consist in driving the car back to this country?'

'No, it didn't.'

'Not? Then why did you have the car searched in Cala Survas?'

Ralph looked at Sterne, worried that he should have fallen in to so obvious a trap.

'Did you know that two cabins were booked at the motel near Lençon by the same person at the same time—yours and cabin number fifty-two?'

'No, I didn't.'

'Who made the booking? The woman who spoke to you at breakfast?'

'I haven't the faintest idea.'

'No one visited you in your cabin?'

'No.'

'But surely someone must have done? You said the container was planted on the Mercedes after Cala Survas. Where else do you suggest it happened if not at the motel?'

'What I mean is, I slept like a log.'

'You're now suggesting that someone entered the garage attached to your cabin when you were fast asleep?'

'All I'm saying is, I was tired and I slept heavily.'

'In the morning, the woman met you in the restaurant and gave you your orders—which were to drive to Calais, cross the Channel on the seven-thirty boat on the Sunday, and stay the night at the motel in Newingreen? She also said that someone would meet you at the motel and collect the car?'

'Yes.'

'She gave you fresh papers for the car, made out in your name?'

'Yes.'

'One last thing. Who are Mr and Mrs K. Smith of seventeen, Riceborough Avenue, Putney?'

'I've no idea.'

'They booked in at the motel in Newingreen on the same night you did.'

Ralph said: 'Why should that fact be of the slightest significance?'

'Because their room was booked at the same time as your brother's and they're the only guests on the night of the fourteenth who gave a false address.'

'That doesn't mean you're entitled to draw a conclusion which involves my brother.'

'Did I forget to mention it?' Young looked surprised. 'The receptionist remembers that at some time Mr Smith asked if your brother had arrived.' Young turned to Sterne. 'Did anyone visit you in your cabin?'

'No.'

'Did anyone go into the garage attached to your cabin?'

'No one came near the cabin or the garage.'

'Your brother will be the first to point out that I can offer you no inducement and can promise you nothing for your full cooperation in this case, but you may like to reflect on the effect that such cooperation could have on the court should the case go to trial.'

'You're inferring . . .' began Ralph.

'I'm inferring nothing. I am saying that it is entirely up to your brother to decide whether he thinks his cooperation will benefit himself.'

Sterne said wildly: 'Cooperate? How the hell can I cooperate more than by telling the truth?'

Ralph leaned forward slightly. 'Who tipped off the police and Customs that an attempt would be made to smuggle drugs through on the night of the fourteenth?'

'I am not aware that I have said there was any such tip-off,' replied Young.

'It wasn't just by chance that all the cars were being searched on arrival at Dover.'

Young made no comment.

'In fact, the container was found in Dover, wasn't it?'

Again, Young remained silent.

'And the Mercedes was followed because you wanted to identify whoever took delivery of the contents of that container. And all the time Angus was at the motel in Newingreen, he was under surveillance?'

Young was a long time in answering, 'Yes.

'His cabin was being watched?'

'Yes.'

'Did the watchers see someone visit him at the cabin?'

'No.'

'Then no one contacted him at the motel.'

'That doesn't follow.'

'It does, unless the watch was inefficient.'

Young's voice became hard. 'When it became obvious that the contents of the container had been passed on, there was an internal investigation to discover whether a good watch had been maintained. It was discovered that there was a period when it probably had not been.'

'When was this?'

'Roughly between two and four in the morning.'

'When Angus was fast asleep.'

'I can't answer as to that.'

'Are you now suggesting that not only was he wide awake, he was also able to judge that the watchers temporarily weren't doing their job so that it was safe for someone to collect something from the container in the car?'

'It's not my job at this stage to suggest anything.'

'But you've been suggesting my brother's guilty of smuggling drugs.'

'I have made no such concrete allegation.'

'He is completely innocent.'

Young leaned back in his chair and stared at Ralph, an expression of quiet contempt on his face. 'When it suits you, you lawyers talk about innocence in hushed, reverent tones. But it means something quite different to you than it does to me. In this case, to me innocence means not guilty of any criminal act. To you, it means guilty by admission of an attempt to evade Common Market tax regulations.'

'You know quite well what I meant by my use of the word. My brother is completely innocent of knowingly smuggling into this country whatever was in the container found in the Mercedes.'

'Knowing is the key word, isn't it?'

'Obviously. So are you investigating all the surrounding circumstances, which must prove he had no knowledge?'

'I am investigating all the surrounding circumstances.'

'Have you found out who owned the Mercedes when it was driven over to the Continent in the first instance?'

'We know who owned it before it was stolen from a car park in south Ruislip on the seventeenth of June. The man concerned has convinced us he can't help our investigations in any way.'

'Have the Spanish police questioned Evans?'

'He left the flat the day after your brother drove away from Cala Survas. No further trace of him has been found.'

'Has the manager of the motel in Lençon been questioned about the booking?'

'It was made by telephone. The registration of a second

cabin was in the name of Mr and Mrs Bressonaud. The address given by them has proved to be false.'

'Did the manager give a description of this couple?'

'He was unable to remember them.'

'He must have remembered something about them.'

'Not necessarily. I understand it's a very busy motel during the season.'

Ralph became silent. Young asked if there were anything more he'd like to know and he answered that there was one more question. Had the traces found in the container yet been analysed?

'I'm afraid not. I've asked the lab boys to hurry things along, but they're under a lot of pressure.'

As, five minutes later, they walked down the spiral ramp to the road, Ralph said, as optimistically as he could: 'We may have gained a very useful point, Angus. The police didn't see anyone entering or leaving your cabin at the Newingreen motel. So how could you have passed on the contents of that container?'

'The superintendent admitted they weren't keeping a proper watch part of the night.'

'Quite. But on top of the point I made at the time, the moment the police can be shown to have been inefficient in any way, a jury begins to wonder how much credence to put in the rest of the police's case.'

'You think they'll arrest me?'

They came to a halt on the edge of the pavement as they waited for the traffic to ease sufficiently to let them cross the road.

'Well?' demanded Sterne.

'It all depends on the analysis of the traces.'

Young and Meacher arrived at Parsonage Farm at eleven-fifteen on Wednesday morning. They informed Sterne that the results of the analysis showed the container had contained heroin, of a 99.5% purity. They arrested him and drove him to divisional HQ where he was taken to the charge room and charged.

CHAPTER 12

The preliminary hearing was held on August 2nd. The case for the prosecution was outlined, prosecution witnesses gave their evidence, were in some cases briefly cross-examined, then were asked to read through their statements and sign them. The eminent QC whom Ralph had briefed for the defence rose to announce, as expected, that the defence reserved their case.

Sterne was committed for trial. The QC asked for bail. The police objected on the grounds that there was reason for believing the accused might try to go abroad to escape trial. The magistrates briefly conferred among themselves and then the chairman said that bail would be allowed on condition that there were two sureties for £10,000 each and the accused surrendered his passport to the police.

Sterne stared out of the opened bedroom window. Everything had changed, yet nothing had changed. He was accused of knowingly smuggling an unknown quantity of heroin into the country and it appeared inevitable he must be found guilty of a crime he had not committed: yet the sun still shone, the trees still stirred to the lazy breeze, and swallows still skimmed overhead.

He gripped his fists until the nails dug into his flesh. Goddam it, he hadn't known about that container so he couldn't be found guilty of knowingly smuggling . . . Yet he'd already learned that innocence and guilt were interpretations, not immutables . . .

Somewhere there had to be proof of his innocence. Yet where? Ralph and his counsel had studied the case for hours, searching for a lead that would help to prove his innocence, and they had found nothing beyond the fact that the police at the Newingreen motel had seen no one enter or leave his cabin. And although Ralph claimed that the admitted slackness of the watchers helped the defence's case, it was obvious it could be argued that it also tended to bolster the prosecution's because now there was no proof that someone had not entered cabin 51 to take delivery . . .

If only Evans could be traced. But Evans had disappeared and any description would be quite useless because around the Mediterranean—was he still in that region?—such a description could fit hundreds of men. What about the woman in the Lençon motel? He'd spoken to her for no more than a few minutes and had learned only that she was as dour as only a charmless, serious, middle-aged woman could be. And from that moment he'd had no further contact with the people who'd organised the running of the car. In fact, apart from Belinda he'd spoken to practically no one . . .

His mind drifted. Ostensibly, Belinda had taken him to the secret gorge to show him how beautiful it was. But it had quickly become clear that it had really been because she had been seeking spiritual healing and reassurance. In this, she'd failed. And when he'd tried to arrange a further meeting, she'd refused to commit herself, even refused to give her address . . . He remembered how she'd looked, at once self-assured and vulnerable, as she'd stood on the pavement and promised to get in touch with him if she felt she wanted to: and so obviously uncertain that she ever would and so embarrassed that she'd abruptly changed the conversation and made small talk about some English car which had just come round the sharp bend . . . The car? He'd looked briefly at it and momentarily it had seemed as if the two men had been surprised by something. Beyond that brief thought, he'd dismissed them and the car from his mind. There'd been no reason for not doing so. Even though she'd remarked that that was the third time they'd seen the car during the day and each time it had been travelling in the opposite direction to them . . . But he knew now that the Mercedes had had hidden about it heroin with a street value of between a third and half a million pounds. Wasn't it reasonable to suppose that those who'd planted this fortune would have wanted to check he was obeying their orders? And hadn't the woman in the restaurant told him to cross the Channel on the Sunday evening, which had meant a good, steady drive so he'd have been expected to leave the motel as soon as he'd finished his breakfast. But he hadn't. And when he had left, he'd had with him Belinda . . . So they'd have kept a very much closer check on him. And without warning he'd turned round and headed back the way he'd come. For them, this must have been panic stations. And then they'd lost him completely. They must have become convinced they'd been double-crossed. But abruptly, as they'd frantically searched this way and that, they'd passed through Vertagne, rounded the last bend in the village, and come on the Mercedes . . .

Excitement seemed to tingle in his throat. Identify the car and there was a lead to the people running the drug-smuggling. It had been a dark blue Rover, almost new. There must be thousands of such Rovers. But Belinda had said its registration letters were the same as her initials . . .

Ralph and Sterne were shown to the interview room by a uniform sergeant who looked as if he'd seen most of what the world had to offer and didn't like any of it.

Young and a second man were standing, a woman sat at the table, notebook open and pen by its side.

'This is Detective-Inspector Parker,' said Young. His voice was sharp, his words clipped. 'Mrs Raight is present to take a full record of everything that is said.'

She had already begun to write in shorthand.

'Since you, Mr Angus Sterne, have been committed to trial, this request for an interview is a most unusual one. The only reason it's been granted is that in the letter it was stated that the matter was of vital importance.'

'It is,' said Ralph.

'Very well.'

Young and Parker sat to the right of Mrs Raight, Ralph and Sterne opposite. Ralph opened his briefcase and brought out some papers. 'My brother has remembered something which should enable you to identify some of the people who are responsible for planting the container on the Mercedes.'

Briefly, Sterne told them about the dark blue Rover.

Young said: 'Am I correct if I say that the sum total of your evidence is that your companion claims to have seen the same car three times, each time heading in an opposite direction to yours, and that on the third occasion you also saw it and it was your impression that the two men in it were unusually interested in you?'

'And the more I think about it, the more certain I am that they'd come round that corner quickly because they were in one hell of a hurry and when they saw the Mercedes the driver instinctively braked, as one would in such circumstances.'

'Suppose you are right in all your suppositions—what steps do you expect us to take?'

'What steps? Trace the car, of course.'

'You have its number?'

'I've told you, only the letters B and B.'

'On such scant . . .'

'Belinda kept noticing the car because its registration letters were the same as her initials. Find out her initials and then it can't be too difficult. I realize that still leaves nine hundred and ninety-nine possibles, but how many of those are going to be dark blue Rovers?'

'You said, find out her initials—do you not know them?'

'I only know her as Belinda Backman.'

'Very well. What is her address?'

'I don't know.'

'For God's sake . . .' Young cut the words short. He looked at Mrs Raight as if wondering whether she'd omit his quick outburst, but as her pen came to a stop he remained silent.

'I've been working things out,' said Sterne urgently. 'She wanted to be put down in Vertagne. She hadn't a penny on her, because she'd lost her handbag along with everything else, so I tried to give her some money but all she'd take were two francs to make a phone call. That means she was near enough to home for two francs, or less, to pay for the call.'

'If the French system is like the British one, two francs could reach a relatively long way for a short time. Who is there at her home?'

'Her mother and stepfather.'

'Is either of them French?'

'Her stepfather is.'

'Then the telephone will be listed under the stepfather's French name and there'll be no way of using a directory to work out possible numbers.'

'It's a case of asking people in the area if they know of a family where a Frenchman is married to an Englishwoman who has a daughter of twenty-three. Foreigners always gain a kind of notoriety.'

'And over how large an area are these inquiries going to have to be made?'

'I'm quite certain she lives near Vertagne because she said that she often went to the gorge.'

'Presumably she has the use of a car?'

'I imagine so. But can't you understand . . .'

'Perhaps it will be best if I explain something. Before I am permitted to forward a request for a foreign police force to carry out inquiries on my behalf, I have to satisfy others that my request is justified by its nature and the facts, and that in practical terms it is fully warranted.'

'It's a fact that the two men in the blue Rover were very surprised to see us.'

'It's an assumption. Even were it more, the work involved in making the search would be such that I'd still not be entitled to ask for it to be undertaken when the only details I can provide are that the lady's name is Belinda Backman and she asked you to drop her in a village called Vertagne.'

'I've said why she must live locally . . .'

'I have to provide the facts, not still more assumptions. And there is yet one more point that needs to be made. Even if this young lady were identified and through her evidence the blue Rover were traced, and even if it turned out to belong to someone who's known to be connected with drug trafficking, these facts would not of themselves establish your innocence of the offence with which you are charged. Your brother will be able to explain the meaning of the term 'knowingly' far more accurately than I: it is with knowingly importing a listed drug that you are charged.'

Young waited a moment; when it was clear nothing more was going to be said, he stood.

Sterne stared up at him. 'What is it?' he demanded bitterly. 'You won't do anything because you're worried Belinda might help me prove my innocence?'

Young's expression became one of contempt.

They sat out on the lawn, in the sunshine, around a glass-topped cane table on which were a plate of thinly cut tomato sandwiches, a chocolate layer cake, cups and saucers, a china teapot, and silver milk jug and bowl.

The more Angela's way of life was threatened, the harder she clung to it.

'Can't you make them understand how terribly important it is to trace Belinda?' she asked.

'God knows, we've tried,' replied Sterne. 'They just wouldn't listen.'

Ralph, who'd been staring at the ancient Bramley tree, said: 'You've got to look at things from their point of view.'

'Why? I'm the bloke in the shit. Look at things from my point of view.'

'Young's bound by rules and regulations.'

'Stuff 'em.'

'When you start talking like that, you're throwing all sense of law and order out of the window.'

'Christ, you're preaching when I'm half an inch away from prison?'

Ralph was hurt by those words. 'All I'm trying to do is explain why he couldn't help you . . . Do you understand the last point he made? That even if the men behind the smuggling are identified through you that doesn't automatically prove you're innocent.'

'If I help to identify them, isn't it goddamn obvious I'm innocent?'

'What is obvious to a policeman is that you may have helped to identify them in order to try to gain a lighter sentence.'

'You think . . .'

'I'm explaining the way their minds work. You've been charged with knowingly importing a prohibited drug. If the circumstances prove that you must have been aware beyond all reasonable doubt that heroin was hidden in the Mercedes, you're guilty. The fact that you've helped the police identify the man who persuaded you to smuggle will count towards mitigation of sentence, nothing more.'

'Just remind me. Are you for the prosecution or the defence?'

Angela said: 'I know it's terribly difficult for you, Angus, but I promise you Ralph is doing everything in his power to help you.' She turned to her husband. 'Can you make it a bit clearer for me? If Belinda can be found and what she says identifies the men behind the smuggling, at the very least that will help Angus get a lesser sentence?'

'Yes.'

'Suppose that because they were identified something then went on to show Angus couldn't have known about the container—wouldn't that prove him innocent?'

Ralph hesitated, looked at his brother, then said quietly: 'If they're identified and arrested and they realize it's because of Angus, they'll do everything they can to hurt him. That means they'll swear blind he knew he was carrying the container and what was in it.'

'Oh! But surely it might just happen in a way that they couldn't do that?'

'I . . . I suppose it might.'

'Then obviously Belinda must be found.'

'Angie, I told you, the police said that they're not in a position to ask the French police to look for her. There's nothing that can be done.'

'Yes, there is. Angus can go to France and find her.'

Ralph stared at her, his expression now one of exasperation. 'You haven't really understood. Angus is on bail and one of the specific conditions of that bail is that he doesn't leave the country.'

'Do conditions like that really count when an innocent man's in danger of being convicted?'

'Of course they do. If Angus is to prove his innocence, he must do so legally—which means, in the courts.'

'And how can he, if he's not allowed to find Belinda? What are you really saying—that observance of form is more important than the providing of justice? Or is it that if the form has been honoured there can, in the eyes of the law, be no injustice?'

He shook his head in further bewilderment. If Angus had argued like this, he would not have been surprised, but that she should . . .

'Ralph, you're far too sensible not to realize that there must be times when one cannot live by the law if there's to be justice.'

'Who decides when such time has come?'

'It's an individual decision.'

'Made subjectively, therefore biased.'

'I don't care how biased. Angus has to go to France to find Belinda since the police won't.'

'If he leaves this country he'll virtually forfeit any chance of proving his innocence . . . Look, I've briefed Reynolds. He's the best man at the bar for this sort of a case.'

'And does he know how to prove Angus innocent?'

Ralph did not answer.

'Angus has to go to France.'

He spoke angrily. 'For God's sake, stop talking nonsense. Angus can't go anywhere because his passport's been impounded.'

'The two of you look so alike that when you're not together you're sometimes mistaken for each other.'

He stared at her, shocked. 'You're suggesting . . .'

'Angus can travel to France on your passport. It's eight years old so the photo of you was taken near enough at the age he is now.'

They'd been married for six years, but this was the first time Ralph had begun to realize that she valued something more highly than her family and reputation.

Ralph paced the bedroom. 'Are you sure you understand the implications of what you're suggesting?'

'I think so,' Angela replied from the bed.

'You're not forgetting how upset you were at the thought of the publicity that would follow if it was discovered that Angus had been attempting a tax fraud? Or how sick it's made you to read in the national press that Angus is accused of drug-running?'

'Of course I haven't forgotten. How could I when I've wanted to crawl away to somewhere where no one's ever heard the name of Sterne?'

He came to a stop by the foot of the bed. 'What you're suggesting now could have far more serious and direct consequences for both of us. I'd be actively helping to break the law and if this was discovered I'd be taken to court. If found guilty—and the verdict couldn't be anything else—I'd almost certainly end up by being struck off the Rolls.'

'All that doesn't change a thing. We have to help Angus prove his innocence.'

He walked round to her side of the bed. 'You know, you're asking me to deny all the precepts by which I've lived and worked and to jeopardize things I hold most dear. Yet I love you for it.' He kissed her.

CHAPTER 13

There was a small queue waiting to pass through emigration and Sterne joined it. The man behind the desk, looking tired, took a passport from a middle-aged woman, thumbed quickly through the first few pages, handed it back. Perhaps, Sterne thought, he'd struck lucky and found someone who was content to do his job with the minimum degree of efficiency . . . But somewhere on the other's desk there must be a list of names and his was probably one of them. And the man might recognize the name of Sterne and look more closely at the photograph in the passport and then at him and he might notice the subtle differences that would be apparent to the trained eye: ears set slightly lower, thicker eyebrows, a different curve to the mouth . . .

Sterne straightened his tie, worn because Ralph would never have travelled in an open neck. Whatever happened, he must remember to answer questions with Ralph's statistics, not his own. Occupation solicitor, not footloose wanderer: place of birth Folkestone, not Maidstone: date of birth May 3rd, not September 17th . . .'

'May I have your passport, please.'

He handed it over. The emigration officer glanced through it, handed it back. 'Next,' he said impatiently.

Sterne walked into the departure lounge. He discovered he'd been sweating heavily.

He left the train at Poitiers. In one corner of the rambling station there was an Avis desk, manned by a woman in the company's neat uniform. She gave him a professional smile and told him he could hire a Renault 5, a Renault 11, a Citröen GS, or a Talbot Alpine. He chose the Renault 11. She asked for passport, driving licence, and credit card.

'I'm paying cash.'

She frowned. 'It becomes difficult,' she said. 'If we have credit cards, we are sure . . .'

Plastic money had really come of age, he thought: it was presumed that only persons of proven creditworthiness would be granted credit cards so someone with one could be more trusted to return the hired car than someone who paid in cash. He opened one of the pockets of his wallet and produced an Access card. 'I'd still rather pay in cash.'

She was satisfied that now everything was in order. She noted the credit card number and then worked out what he owed for a seven-day hire.

*

It had all seemed so straightforward and simple when he'd spoken to Young. Belinda must live within a local telephone call of Vertagne and so all that was needed was to ask around about a family where the husband was French, the mother English, and the twenty-three-year-old daughter of the mother's first marriage was tall and fairly slim and had chestnut, curly hair and dark brown eyes . . .

The small boulangerie and pâtisserie in the square at Vertagne was still filled with the heady scent of bread baked for the midday meal. He bought a ficelle and two éclairs and then tried to ask the woman about Belinda. But because he was no longer buying, she no longer understood his fractured French.

He walked down the street to find, a hundred metres along, an old-fashioned general store which sold food, wine, vegetables, and many kinds of kitchen dry goods. There were three kinds of pâté in a small chilled unit and he chose the pepper one. The woman, middle-aged, plump, and garrulous, cut him a generous slice and wrapped it up with great care. He added a two-hundred-gramme pack of butter, a bottle of vin ordinaire, and a kitchen knife, to his purchases and paid. As he pocketed the change, he said that his fiancée was staying with friends near the village, but he'd suddenly discovered that he'd lost her address: did she know of a family where the husband was French and the wife and her daughter were both English? In halting French the story sounded weaker than ever, but the woman was a romantic and not prepared to be critical. She rested her plump elbows on the counter by the side of a bowl of cooked chick-peas and began to list all the families in which there were foreigners. Unfortunately, it became clear that a foreigner was someone who came from beyond the district.

He returned to the car, left the village, and turned down the first lane. He picnicked by a circle of poplars, enjoying the view over rolling, wooded countryside and the pâté which was nearly as good as the woman in the shop had claimed.

Twenty minutes later he drove into Bardineaux and parked outside the town hall, marked by the Tricolor hanging over the pretentious, columned entrance to the tall, square building. He talked to one man who suggested he spoke to another, who suggested he spoke to a third. The third man was tall and long-faced, with a small moustache and he looked not unlike de Gaulle: however, his manner was gracious and helpful and he spoke a reasonable form of English. If Monsieur Sterne would like to wait, he would see what he could find out . . .

When he returned, he regretfully said that the records he'd consulted failed to list any family living in the district where the husband was French, the mother and daughter English.

By seven-thirty, Sterne finally admitted that there was no point in continuing the search that day. Few shops were still open, public offices had long since closed, and the last person to whom he'd spoken had made it perfectly clear that the state of her cooking was far more important than the extent of his troubles. He parked in front of the Auberge du Mail in Recour and went inside to ask if there was a room free. The woman he spoke to wanted to know if he'd be eating dinner there and when he said he would she decided there was a room free. She led him up a staircase—split down the centre so one hopped from side to side to ascend it—and along a crooked corridor to a large room, scrupulously clean, filled with furniture that would have delighted the heart of any collector of rural antiques. He said the room was fine, she said that dinner would be served at eight-thirty and the bisque d'homard was a dream. She showed him where the bathroom was, then left, presumably to return to the kitchen and complete the preparation of the dream soup.

He washed away the day's travelling grime, returned to the bedroom, sat on the bed, and spread out a map. He'd dropped Belinda at Vertagne. If his theory was right, she lived somewhere near there. But how near was near? He'd searched the map for the secret gorge and, after some difficulty, had finally decided where it was and had marked it with a cross. Because this position was south of Vertagne, he'd so far concentrated his inquiries to the south. But as Young had pointed out, if Belinda had travelled to the gorge by car, it could virtually be in any direction and at any distance . . . Yet she'd first been taken there when she was sixteen. She wouldn't have held a driving licence at that age. So wasn't it reasonable to accept that to begin with she'd reached it either on a bicycle or moped? . . . He was convinced she lived within 15 kilometres of the gorge, however arbitary that figure was. He measured 15 kilometres and, the gorge as the centre, drew a rough circle of that radius. He was disheartened to note how many towns and villages lay within it.

By Thursday afternoon, his feeling was more one of despair than disheartenment. Mostly his inquiries had met a blank, but occasionally he'd been given information which had sent him hurrying on, certain that this time he'd finally found Belinda. In this way, he'd met an American couple who were soon returning to Rockford, Illinois, and hoped he'd visit them there; a Dutchman married to a doe-eyed Indonesian who'd looked at him with an expression in her soft brown eyes which had disturbed him even though he couldn't translate it; and two Englishwomen who lived in a tumbledown cottage and who were, so the elder of them assured him, artists of genius, awaiting the recognition which must one day be accorded them: and would he like to buy one of their paintings for only five hundred francs? . . .

He backed down the potholed dirt track to the metalled road and retraced his route to the crossroads. Looking for a needle in a haystack was child's play by comparison with what he was trying to do, he thought bitterly. He'd made certain assumptions, based on little more than guesswork, and these could be hopelessly wrong. Even if they were only slightly wrong—for instance, if Belinda lived within 20 kilometres of the gorge, not 15, then the area became so great that it was ridiculous to imagine he had any chance of success . . .

He passed a signpost marked Brillant and he remembered that this was the village beyond which they'd turned off to go to the gorge. Abruptly, he decided to visit it and see if its quiet, contemplative beauty could chase away his bitter sense of failure.

At the crossroads past the small village, he turned into the dead straight, rising lane which became lost in the distant trees. He breasted the hill and reached the T-junction, turned into the very narrow lane with its high earth banks. Further on he made a sharp left turn, passed beyond the trees, and continued up to the final right-hand bend which brought him on to the very small plateau. A car was already parked there. He swore. He'd come seeking peace and what he'd found was, like as not, a family outing with a horde of screaming children. Secret gorge? It might as well have been listed in Michelin with a little red <s

The Citröen CX was parked in the centre of the plateau so that it left him insufficient room to turn. Then to leave, he had to find the driver and ask him to move the Citröen. He climbed out, slammed the door shut with unnecessary force.

Despite his sense of annoyance, the peace began to wash over him. Birds resumed singing and amongst them there were the crystal clear notes of a nightingale. The distant murmur of water on rocks was a lullaby. And no screaming children as yet. He started down the natural path. A humming-bird hawk-moth, its wings thrumming, hovered in front of a cowslip bell: a large grasshopper launched itself forward just before his right foot would have crushed it: a dragonfly soared away with a banking turn.

He saw movement to his left. Wearing a red blouse and a cotton skirt, a woman was making her way up to where he stood. When she drew nearer, he recognized Belinda.

CHAPTER 14

He stood and stared at her round, piquant, character-filled face. 'I've been scouring the countryside for days for you.'

She came to a stop a few feet from him, beyond a ragged clump of cistus.

'I've asked in every town and village in the area, but no one had ever heard of you. So I came here to try and restore my shattered morale.'

'And found me. If you were a man of any faith, you'd have known this would happen. This isn't just a secret gorge, it's a magic one as well.' She came forward a couple of paces, then sat. He settled by her. 'I heard a car arrive and the door slam and I cursed the intruder,' she continued. 'I called on the gods of the gorge to make him trip over his feet, fall, and break his neck. I'm glad they weren't listening.'

'And I saw the Citröen and cursed and imagined a stout, puffing father, a harassed mother, and a horde of screaming children. I didn't call on the gods to rid me of them because I didn't know about the gods then, but I would have done if I had.'

She reached out and picked a long stalk of grass. 'I've been here a lot recently. I just couldn't decide what to do.' She nibbled the grass. Then she said, in a distant dreamy voice: 'When I got back home both my mother and Jean were so pleased to see me that it made me feel quite humble—and that's not something I'm used to feeling. I told them what had happened with the two Italians and Jean . . . I've always thought he could be a hard, even cruel man, but I'll swear that if he'd got hold of those two he'd have killed them . . . Neither of them so much as hinted at the fact that if I'd stayed at home instead of being a fool and going off with Michel, none of it would ever have happened . . . They only reproached me when I said how I'd made you drop me at Vertagne and that was why Jean had had to pick me up there. They were angry because I hadn't brought you home for them to thank you for all you'd done for me . . . But you understood, didn't you?'

'I'm not sure that I did.'

'Or was it your masculine ego that was hurt?' Her smile robbed the words of any malice. 'Shall I tell you what it was I couldn't decide? Whether or not to get in touch with you again. And minutes before you arrived here, I came to a decision.'

'Which was?'

'What's it matter now?'

'Maybe masculine ego would like to know that we'd have met again a bit later on, if not by pure chance now.'

'Pure chance? We meet here, in my secret gorge, and you can call it pure chance? That's sacrilege. If you don't apologize right away, something terrible will happen.'

'Apologize to whom?'

'The gods of the gorge, of course. After all, they

arranged for us to come here at the same time. Come on, apologize.'

'I have.'

'At the top of your voice, so they can hear you.'

'Deaf—that sounds ungodlike?'

'Please, Angus.'

Feeling somewhat foolish, he begged the gods' pardon for having doubted their responsibility for this meeting.

'That's better.'

The quality of the light altered and she looked up. 'The sun's just gone behind the other bank, so it'll soon start to get a bit chilly—even at this time of the year one can need a sweater. So we'd better move.'

He stood and held out his hand to help her to her feet. When they reached the small plateau and the cars, she said: 'I'll move so you can get round, then you lead the way down the lane. When we reach the main road, turn right and I'll come past you and lead the way.'

'Where are we heading for?'

'Home.'

She moved the Citröen as far as she dared and this left him just enough room in which to manœuvre. When he reached the main road he turned right and continued slowly in second, watching his rear-view mirror. The Citröen appeared, drew out, and passed him to the accompaniment of a quick bleep of the horn.

They continued on the main road for several kilometres, then carried on through a series of side roads until the Citröen began to slow, with left indicator flashing. He looked past the Citröen and saw a high brick wall in which was set a wide gateway with intricately designed and executed wrought-iron gates.

He'd often wondered about her background. She'd been too emotionally disturbed for him to judge from her behaviour, her clothes had been those of a wanderer, she'd worn no jewellery, and had lost all her personal possessions, yet nevertheless he'd gained the definite impression that she came from a comfortable background. He had not imagined a luxurious one.

Beyond the gates was a parkland setting, with specimen trees, English in character. In contrast the house was wholly French. Beautifully proportioned, with two main floors and a third one set slightly back, and a small round tower at either end of the front façade, it was built of honey-coloured stone and had a slate roof. On either side of the bronze front-door were stone statues of voluptuous females, bearing cornucopias on their shoulders. In the centre of the turning circle at the end of the drive was a lily pool, holding long, lazy golden carp.

Two borzois came round the far side of the house and barked until she'd left the Citröen to stroke them. Their barking recommenced when he climbed out of the Renault.

'Shut up! This is Angus Sterne and from now on he's your friend. D'you understand?'

The borzois studied Sterne and barked more loudly.

'They're just bad-mannered. Ignore them and evenutally they'll be quiet.' She came over to him and linked her arm with his. 'Before we go in, you'll answer one question. Why did you drive so slowly when you reached the main road?'

'To let you get by.'

'Was that the only reason? And you're on your honour to confess the truth.'

'Well . . . maybe I was also making quite sure.'

'That I didn't shoot off in the opposite direction and try to lose you? I thought so! Don't you understand that since the gods of the gorge had decided we should meet again, I could never do a thing like that?'

She was speaking facetiously, yet he knew that at heart she was not being wholly facetious.

Her mother and stepfather were in the family sitting-room, a small, pleasantly informal room which, as he learned later, was in sharp contrast to the drawing-room. Evelyn was handsome in a mature, sophisticated manner and she was dressed in clothes which had all the elegant simplicity of expert design and dressmaking: her few pieces of jewellery were choice. Jean de Matour was of medium height thick in build, and like his wife's, his clothes, though his were informal, had the unmistakable stamp of expensive quality. His face was round and regularly featured and he smiled a lot, showing two gold-capped teeth. He seemed a naturally charming man. Yet even on this first meeting, when he came under the scrutiny of the cool grey-green eyes, Sterne immediately remembered how Belinda had spoken of him as someone very kind and considerate, yet at the same time of very strong character and probably capable of cruelty.

'This is Angus Sterne,' said Belinda.

Evelyn exclaimed with surprise, then turned to Sterne. 'If you only knew how many times I've told Belinda that it was absolutely unforgivable to make you drop her at Vertagne and not ask you back here so that we could thank you.'

De Matour grasped Angus's right hand in both of his and pumped it up and down. 'It's an honour,' he said, his English good, his choice of words slightly archaic. 'It is also a very great pleasure. As Evelyn says, it was a dreadful thing to do. Again and again we ask Belinda to tell us your address so that we might write and give you our thanks, but always she says she does not have it.' He turned to Belinda. 'I think perhaps, that was not quite true?'

'Perhaps.'

He turned back. 'How does one apologize for one's children when one has no control over them?'

'One doesn't try,' Belinda said. She went up to her stepfather and kissed him on the cheek. 'One just continues to spoil them abominably.'

'Then the fault is really ours,' he said, with mock contrition. 'But now we must change the mood and drink a welcome of thanks, even if for an Englishman the sun has not yet descended past the . . . What is the word?'

'Yard-arm,' said Evelyn.

'Of course: I am getting old and forget, but that is one of the privileges of old age: that and the right to a kiss on the cheek from a beautiful woman. Angus—as an old man I must surely be allowed yet one more privilege: that of calling an Englishman by his Christian name before I have known him for ten years—do you like champagne? I have a friend who each year sends me some cases of his finest champagne which I keep for special occasions.'

Because he had not been expected, Evelyn told Sterne, dinner was unfortunately only very simple. Simple, Sterne thought, as he started on his second helping of veal cutlets in a truffle sauce, was a word which meant different things to different people.

When they'd finished eating, Belinda and Evelyn left the dining-room. De Matour crossed to the ornately inlaid sideboard and picked up a heavy silver cigar box. 'It is perhaps treason for a Frenchman to observe an English custom, nevertheless I freely admit to enjoying regularly a cigar and a glass of port after dinner without female company to disturb and dilute the pleasure. Will you join me in both?'

'The port with pleasure, but not the cigar.'

De Matour carried a crystal decanter over to the table. 'If I may be permitted to sit here, instead of at the end of the table? . . . Now comes the eternal problem. In which direction does tradition dictate that I pass the port? I always forget.'

'Port's red, the red sidelight of a ship is on the left-hand side.'

'But that requires an elderly man with a muddled mind to remember which side of a ship is the port side.'

Sterne doubted that de Matour's brain was in the slightest degree muddled.

They filled their glasses and drank. Sterne was not surprised to discover that the port was of a quality he had only once before met. De Matour lit his cigar with care, removing the band, using a cutter with finicky precision, striking a non-safety match, and holding the end of the cigar in the flame until it was sufficiently alight for him to draw on it. He leaned back in his chair. 'Words, Angus, can be annoying tools. They were designed to enable us to express our feelings, but so often they fall down on their task—or it it that we have become too civilized to use them honestly? Civilization and emotions do not make good bedfellows. Nevertheless, I will try to express to you our very deep feelings of gratitude for all that you did for Belinda. It was the act of a man of great honour.'

'Anyone else would have done the same,' said Sterne, slightly uncomfortable because of the emotional intensity with which de Matour had spoken.

'By no means.' He suddenly relaxed and chuckled. 'The English really are very vulnerable to words. One has only to use them with deep sincerity and stiff upper lips shiver with embarrassment . . . So now let me compound that embarrassment by discussing money. My excuse is that only an uneducated Frenchman would be guilty of so criminal a faux pas. You bought Belinda some clothes and paid for her motel room. Please tell me the total cost to you so that I may repay you.'

Sterne did not make the mistake of trying to say that there was no need for repayment. He thought for a moment, then said: 'As near as I can work it out, three hundred francs.'

De Matour brought out a crocodile-skin wallet from the breast pocket of his coat. He couted out three one-hundred-franc notes and passed these over. 'Now, our business is concluded and I have no further reason to cause you embarrassment. So we may enjoy ourselves and when this is appropriate, refill our glasses.'

Twenty minutes later they left the dining-room and went through to the sitting-room. Belinda said she was feeling stifled and would Sterne join her in a walk outside?

They left via the french windows. The moon was full and they could see clearly enough to walk across the grass.

'I hope the after-dinner ritual wasn't too ghastly?' she asked.

'Far from it.'

'Jean's a sweetie, but he does have some odd ideas: he thinks the upper crust in England still finish every dinner with the port ritual so he religiously observes it here.'

'Aren't you being a bit bitchy?'

She tucked her arm round his. 'I've said it to his face and I've never seen a man laugh so much. He's got a tremendous sense of humour and can always laugh at himself. That's one of the reasons I like him so much.'

'He seems . . . well, a strange mixture.'

'He's that, all right. He's a terrible snob, but he's never contemptuous of other people: he's selfish, but can't do too much for Evelyn: he's contemptuous of weakness, but always tries to help me: I'm sure he can be hard, even cruel, yet he's also so kind it's incredible . . . The strangest thing of all is, I've absolutely no idea what he did before he married Evelyn. I've asked him point blank and he's turned the question aside with a shrug and a smile . . . He's so wealthy that I think he must have been mixed up in something tough and very illegal.'

'I expect you'll find he was in nothing more criminal than the stock exchange.'

'Then he'd say so.'

'Some people have sufficient self-respect to keep that sort of connection to themselves.'

They walked for a while, then she came to a stop. 'Angus, will you tell me something?'

'If I can.'

'What's worrying you?'

'Who said anything was?'

'You don't have to spell it out,' she said impatiently. 'All evening while you've been making small talk and behaving like the perfect guest, the look's been in your eyes. Why?'

He resumed walking and, since their arms were still linked, she perforce had to do the same.

'Are you going to tell me?' she demanded.

'I've been thinking that I was a fool to come here with you.'

'That . . . that's a beastly thing to say.' She jerked her arm free.

'I don't mean I regret for one second being with you.'

'Then what in the hell do you mean?'

'You've a home that's a shield against the nastiness of the world. I'm scared I may turn that shield.'

'I don't understand what on earth you're saying.'

He told her briefly what had happened in England.

'The police think you knew you were smuggling in heroin?'

'Yes.'

'Can't they judge a man?'

'As far as they're concerned I'm obviously capable of having known. After all, I was trying to evade the car tax.'

'For God's sake, there's no connection between the two.'

'There is to them.'

'What bloody stupid fools people can be.'

They came to a post-and-rail fence and she rested her arms on the top rail. 'Angus, would you have tried to find me if you hadn't needed to know my initials?'

'Of course.'

She touched his arm in a brief gesture of pleasure.

From some way away, a tawny owl hooted. Their attention was caught by a nearby rustle in the grass, but the moonlight was not quite strong enough for them to see what caused it. A bulling cow blared its monotonous love-call.

'Well, aren't you going to ask me what my initials are?'

'What are they?'

'Abigail Belinda Dorothy Backman. Anyone who calls me Abigail is off my visiting list for ever.'

'And Dorothy?'

'It inevitably gets shortened to Dotty and that's too close to the truth for comfort.'

'So the registration of the car was A three numbers BDB; Any idea what the numbers were?'

'None at all.'

'The police can surely still trace the car.'

'So what are you going to do now?'

He turned and stared directly at her and he thought that the moonlight softened her face so that she became beautiful as well as attractive, but at the same time it robbed her of some character. 'I'm faced with the next-to-impossible—proving a negative. So I've been wondering if anyone at the motel in Lençon can tell me anything that would help. I think I'll go and find out. I know the French police questioned the staff, but it won't have been in any depth.'

'First of all, you'll have to visit the gorge and ask the gods for help.'

He wished he could believe it might be that easy.

He telephoned England just after ten o'clock.

Ralph was clearly in a state of high tension. 'What's been happening? I expected to hear from you days ago. What's gone wrong?'

'Nothing's wrong. Thing's have just taken a long time. I've found Belinda and her initials are ABDB. So pass them on to the police and they'll trace the Rover.'

'For God's sake, start thinking. I can't do that all the time you're in France or they'll put two and two together and be waiting for you when you try to return. Are you coming back tomorrow?'

'No. I'm hanging on here for a little.'

'You're what? Angus, don't you understand, you're sitting on a powder keg all the time you're there on my passport?'

'I'm not going to find the proof I need to clear me back in England, am I?'

There was a long pause.'No, you're not,' Ralph said.

CHAPTER 15

After breakfast, eaten outside on the south terrace, Sterne said: 'I hope you won't mind if I pack and leave right away?'

Evelyn, surprised, even slightly put out, said: 'I was expecting you to stay for at least a few days. I've already asked Cook to prepare a special dinner for tonight.'

'That makes it twice as difficult to go. But I'm afraid I must.'

'There's no way in which we can persuade you to change your mind?' asked de Matour.

'I wish there were.'

'Then we'll just have to try and do justice on your behalf to the dinner.'

'There's still time for a change of plans,' said Evelyn. 'If Angus isn't going to be here, we'll go back to having a simple meal.'

De Matour spoke lugubriously. 'You see, Angus, how

sadly your early departure affects us all. You deprive Cook of the satisfaction of preparing a superb dinner and me of the even greater satisfaction of eating it. And when you reach my age, the pleasures of the table tend to be the only ones one is able to enjoy to any degree.'

'You're just plain greedy,' said Evelyn.

'Indeed. But what is the point in employing a superb cook if one is not greedy? . . . Angus, you must promise to return here as soon as possible and to stay for very much longer.'

'The moment I can.' Sterne tried, and failed, to speak lightly.

De Matour looked briefly at him with sharp curiosity.

Sterne stood. 'So if you'll excuse me, I'll go and do my bit of packing.' He left.

Evelyn turned. 'Belinda, do you think . . .'

'Sorry, but I'm in a hurry.' She pushed back her chair. 'I'd better throw something into a case because I don't know how long we'll be away.'

They watched her hurry into the house.

'When I was young,' remarked de Matour, 'it was considered necessary to give one's parents sufficient notice if one wished to go away. They needed time in which to decide whether they approved of one's going.'

'Different ages, different customs.'

'Clearly. But I can't prevent myself being envious.'

When Sterne came down the curving staircase, with its banisters of delicate wrought-iron, Evelyn and de Matour were waiting. He thanked them for their hospitality.

'No, no!' de Matour said forcefully. 'It is for us to say thank you with all our hearts . . .'

'He knows how we feel,' interrupted Evelyn. 'The trouble with you French is you will try to make a meal out of everything. Why not let some things speak for themselves.'

'Perhaps, my dear, because we do not enjoy the British

love of ambiguity.'

'Nonsense . . . Angus, remember: you're to come back just as soon as you can.'

'That's a promise,' Sterne answered. 'Have you any idea where Belinda is so I can say goodbye?'

'But I thought . . .' She looked at her husband, who shrugged his shoulders.

There were the sounds of a car and they turned to look through the window. They saw the Renault 11, driven by Belinda, brake to a halt.

'She's brought the car round for me,' said Sterne. 'Well, thanks again and goodbye.'

'Au revoir,' corrected de Matour.

They watched him leave, reach the car, and then, quite clearly, have an argument with Belinda. De Matour said: 'When I was young, I may have been irresponsible, but I always knew when a young lady was accompanying me on my travels.'

As they drove along the busy N road, Belinda said: 'What's your plan of campaign when we get there?'

'Have a word with the manager about the couple who booked the other cabin. And if he can't help, talk to the rest of the staff.'

'What exactly are you hoping to discover?'

He shook his head. 'I'm damned if I know.'

'Then how will you be certain if you find it?'

'I don't know that either. Bloody silly, isn't it?'

She lit a cigarette. 'Would it help if you can find someone who saw the other couple going into the garage of your cabin?'

'Only if that someone could also swear I was fast asleep and unaware of what was going on.'

'But . . . but there's not much chance of that, is there?'

'No.'

'Then it's . . .'

'Hopeless? Probably. But I'll always know I've done everything I could. And at least I found you and through you the registration letters of the blue Rover.'

'Which as far as I can make out won't necessarily help you.'

'From the charge of knowingly importing the heroin? No, it won't.'

'Angus, I don't want to sound pessimistic, but . . . but if the worst comes to the worst, don't go back to England. Stay here, in France.'

'I'm afraid that would land Ralph in it, right up to his eyebrows. And how long would I be allowed to stay free? The English police would put a request through to the French police and I'd be scooped up, no trouble.'

'They wouldn't, not if you stayed with us.'

'Your mother and Jean aren't going to welcome a drug-smuggler on the lam.'

She spoke angrily. 'They've both got far too much judgement to begin to believe you could ever have done something like that, knowing what you were doing.'

'They might begin by believing me. But after a while . . .? They'd remember the old adage—no smoke without fire.'

They reached the motel at a quarter past five and he parked behind a Spanish registered Seat. He was about to open his door, when she said: 'Angus.'

He let go of the door-handle. 'Yes?'

'What are you booking? One room or two?'

'Two, of course,' he answered, his tone sharp.

'Why?'

'Isn't that obvious?'

'Only if you think I'm not worth the effort of bedding.'

'If you don't know what I think, you're stupid.'

'The day my last headmistress and I finally and thankfully parted, she said that if only I'd ever bothered to work I might have done quite well. So I think I must be lazy, but not stupid.'

'You're being lazy now. Start using your brains.'

'With me, brains always come second to emotions.'

'Goddamn it, you're not making it easy for me.'

'I'm not trying to.' She rested her left arm along the back of his seat and ran her fingers across his neck. 'Why should you have everything your way?'

'Pack that in.'

'You don't like your neck being stroked? . . . Oh dear, perhaps you're gay?'

He swore.

She said, almost angrily: 'You're in trouble and you can't see a way out of it. That's why you're trying to hold me at arm's length, isn't it? Well, who asked you to be so bloody self-sacrificing?'

'If I can't find out anything . . .'

'You'll return to England because you're honourable and wouldn't dream of letting your brother down.'

'Is that so extraordinary?'

'It's wonderful. But I'm not going to let your honour deprive me of my happiness.'

'Happiness? Knowing what's got to come?'

'Yes.'

'I'm booking two rooms.'

'You're booking one,' she corrected.

The manager of the motel was an Englishman's idea of the typical Frenchman: short, round-faced, balding, a funny little moustache, a generous stomach, and an inability to fill his clothes smartly. He stood behind the desk in the small, cluttered office which lay behind the reception desk. 'I no understand,' he said, in heavily accented English.

Belinda spoke for the first time, her French fluent and fast, her r's rolled with Parisian élan.

The manager shook his head. 'Madame, I regret that I

do not remember these guests.'

'They booked two rooms, one for themselves, one for Monsieur Sterne, for Friday, July the twelfth.'

'So you have already said. But we have a large number of guests throughout the summer . . .'

'It might help if you took the trouble to check your records.'

'It can make no difference. As I told the police when they asked me, I cannot remember guests who stay here only one night and who, in any case, I probably never see.'

'Madame Bressonaud was probably middle-aged, had a heavy, square face, wore horn-rimmed glasses, and dressed badly in a pleated, check skirt that was too short for her.'

'I'm sorry,' said the manager, 'but I remember no one of that description. And now, as I'm a very busy man, perhaps you'd be kind enough to leave me to my work?'

'How were the reservations made?'

'Madame, without wasting a great deal of time searching through the books, I cannot answer.'

'The least you can do . . .' she began.

'Forget it,' interrupted Sterne.

As soon as they were out of earshot, she said: 'Why d'you give in like that?'

'Because you were about to blow your top and we weren't getting anywhere.'

'Goddamnit! . . . I was so hoping he'd be able to tell us something.' She gripped his hand tightly. 'What are we going to do now?'

'Find the chambermaid who'd have been responsible for the cabin and see if she can help.'

'If she's like him, she won't even tell us the time.'

'A hundred-franc note may persuade here to be more forthcoming.'

The sight of the hundred-franc note made the angular,

toothy, bony woman very forthcoming, but it soon became evident that she was not able to help. 'I seem to remember her, yes . . . Couldn't stop wondering how she could dress so terribly. I mean, being so fat in something like that!'

'The couple gave a false address. Did you learn anything to suggest where they really came from?'

'Nothing like that. When I spoke to her it was just to make certain everything was all right. The manager don't like the staff getting familiar with guests.'

'What did the husband look like?'

She thought back. 'I don't remember seeing him.'

'But he was around?'

'Next morning both beds needed changing and making, if that's what you mean?'

'What luggage was there?'

'There was a suitcase. There'd have to be, wouldn't there?'

'Just one?'

She shrugged her shoulders.

'Did you get a chance to see what was in the suitcase?'

'Here, you're not suggesting . . .'

'We're not suggesting anything except that a suitcase might have been open when you were in the cabin.'

'It wasn't.'

'That's about it, then,' said Sterne, as he handed the chambermaid the hundred-franc note.

'There's just one more question.' Belinda turned to speak to the chambermaid again. 'Can you think of anyone else who might have talked to either of them and so be able to help us?'

The chambermaid shook her head. 'They were in my rooms, so no other staff would go in unless it was the plumber or carpenter and there wasn't no call for either of them.' She paused, then smirked. 'Of course, maybe Pierre saw something.'

'Pierre?'

'He was the odd-job man on night duty.' She giggled. 'He was too odd, which is why he got the sack.'

'How d'you mean?'

'The old bastard . . . Oh, I'm sorry. I mean, the manager turned up unexpectedly the other night and caught him looking.'

'Looking at what?'

'Into the cabins . . . He'd bored holes through the walls of some of 'em so he could see what the guests were up to.'

'It's just as well he got the sack before last night,' Sterne said to Belinda.

CHAPTER 16

Lençon was divided by the river Lence into two unequal parts. To the north and east was the old and much smaller section with narrow streets, steep-roofed houses with eaves, and a cathedral which was Norman in origin but had been heavily altered in the middle of the seventeenth century. Once the centre of considerable commercial activity, the area had declined as the new section to the south and west of the river had grown until now it was little more than a district of slums.

Pierre Foucarde lived on the third floor of a house which looked as if it must collapse unless steps were taken to shore it up. He was a large, heavily built man with hands that were noticeable small in proportion and elegant. His round, open face expressed sly good humour. His voice was thick with the local accent, many of the consonants being completely lost, so that occasionally Belinda had some difficulty in understanding him. If he felt the slightest sense of shame at having been sacked from the motel for being a Peeping Tom, this never

became apparent.
'Room fifty-two?' He crossed to a battered desk which stood beyond the head of the single bed and brought from this a large notebook. He returned to the rush-bottomed chair which rocked slightly every time he shifted his weight. 'What day d'you say?'
'Friday, July the twelfth.'
'He turned the pages of the notebook. 'Fifth . . . Eighth . . . Here we are.'
'My God!' Belinda said in English, 'he's kept a diary.'
'Tomorrow's best seller,' replied Sterne. '*Tropic of Lençon*.'
Foucarde patiently waited until they had finished speaking, then he said: 'Yeah, I had a look in cabin fifty-two.'
'At what time?'
'Just after eleven.'
'What did you see?'
'There was a lady in bed, reading. She wasn't pretty: all lumpy, know what I mean?'
'And her husband?'
'There wasn't no one else in the room.'
'Are you sure? A couple booked in.'
Foucarde checked his notebook, shook his head. 'There was only her . . . And . . .' He scratched his head. 'Seems like I remember her clothes was on the second bed.'
Belinda said to Sterne: 'If she put her clothes on the other bed, it wasn't going to be used. So where on earth had the husband got to?'
'The chambermaid said both beds had been slept in, but I'm beginning to wonder if they really were. Maybe the husband never was around and it was only made to seem he was.'
She questioned Foucarde once more. 'How much of the bedroom could you see?'
He answered at length, proud to detail his skills. The

hole had been bored through the concrete-block wall months before and into this he'd inserted the small viewer which consisted of two strong lenses set in a thin copper tube: this gave a magnified view of part of the room with a good focus in the centre but rapidly distorting vision towards the periphery. If he'd not been caught by the manager when he had, he'd been going to build a second and much better viewer which would have cut out much of the distortion—sadly, the action had so often taken place where the distortion was great.

'Was there a metal container, roughly a quarter of a metre long and ten centimetres wide and deep, anywhere in the room?'

'I didn't see one.'

As they stepped out of the building on to the pavement, Belinda said: 'After that, I feel I need a bath, hair wash, and mouth rinse. God, I'll never feel safe in a hotel room again.'

'Use them just for sleeping in.'

She linked her arm with his, gaining a sense of reassurance from the physical contact. They walked down the sloping, cobbled road and reached the T-junction to the right of which they'd left the Renault. He unlocked the doors and they climbed in.

'He didn't help, did he?' she asked.

'No.'

She lit a cigarette. 'So what do we do now?'

'I don't think there's really anything more we can do. No one saw the container in the woman's possession, no one saw her enter the garage of my cabin while I was fast asleep . . . Nothing's changed.'

'But you didn't know what was happening.'

'I didn't. But I can't prove that negative.'

'Stop sounding so defeatist.'

'Suggest something to do and I'll do it. Otherwise I am defeated.'

'I . . . I'm sorry, my darling. But I just can't bear to see . . .' She stopped.

'To see the inevitable drawing nearer all the time.' He turned to look at her and saw she was crying.

She buried her face in the crook of his neck and as he put his arm round her he felt her shaking. A couple of elderly women, carrying shopping baskets, stared curiously at them as they walked past the car.

'I'm sorry,' she said, her voice muffled. 'And that's the second time I've said sorry—normally I never do.'

'Then at least we're making progress in one direction.'

'Pig!' She nibbled his neck, then sat upright. 'I'm all right now and I won't apologize for anything more. Let's get out of here and have a drink and a meal and forget everything but ourselves and now.'

Normally a man who prided himself on a good sense of direction, he twice lost his way among the narrow, twisting streets, but finally they came to the most westerly of the three bridges across the Lence.

'Take the Perigueux road. I know of a restaurant that's not in Michelin because the proprietor's a tremendous character who takes sharp likes and dislikes and if he dislikes you he serves you poor food so you don't come back. But if he likes you, the food's three stars plus. I've only been there twice, but he seemed to like me and he told me how to prepare two of the dishes.'

'So you're not only lovely, you're a good cook to boot?'

'I'm too impatient to be a good cook, but one day I'll pull myself together and cook the two dishes for you.'

There was a silence.

'Say something, can't you?' she demanded fiercely, 'even if it's only to tell me I'm a one night stand and last night was my night.'

'Do you need it spelled out?'

'Yes, I bloody well do.'

'If I could, I'd marry you tomorrow.'

'Why can't you?'

'What the hell would it look like for you to be married to a convicted dope-smuggler?'

'You're innocent.'

'The outside world doesn't care about guilt and innocence, only appearances: and my appearance is guilty.'

They passed beyond the outskirts of the town and for a short time drove parallel with the river, now wide and shallow and overhung by willows. Then the river curved away.

'Belinda,' he said, 'it's no good hoping thing'll change, as if this was just a bad dream. They won't. Before long, I've got to return home and appear in court. The QC who's defending me has given it straight from the shoulder. Unless fresh evidence comes to light, there's no chance of my escaping a heavy prison sentence.

'Originally, I thought that identification of the blue Rover must provide the fresh evidence which would clear me, but the detective-superintendent soon scotched that one. I've got to do more than identify the people behind the smuggling—I've got to prove I didn't know that the Mercedes, when it entered Dover, had a quantity of heroin hidden in it.'

'Maybe . . .' She became silent.

'Miracles don't happen these days. They disappeared along with saints.'

The restaurant lay half a kilometre up a lane and it was set on high ground so that diners had a distant view over lush countryside. The building was a solid, chunky farmhouse, faced with the local grey stone that might have added a sense of dourness but for the colourful garden and the vine-covered outside patio. The proprietor was the chef, his wife kept the till and bar, and their daughter was the waitress. Meals could take a long time to prepare, but anyone stupid enough to complain was told to leave and drive to the nearest hamburger joint. The cellar was not extensive, but it was highly selective and it was possible to buy a superb but little-known wine at half the price one would have paid for a bottle of Romanée-Conti.

As he warmed a glass of armagnac in the palm of his hand, Sterne asked: 'Who was it said, "Let me die now, O Lord, when I have supped of heaven"?'

'I don't know,' Belinda answered, 'and what's more I don't bloody care.' She stubbed out a cigarette, picked up her glass, and finished the Cointreau in one quick swallow.

'Don't forget, it was you who said we had to live for ourselves and now.'

'All right, it was me, so for the third time today, I'm sorry, I'm spoiling a wonderful meal, but I can't stop thinking . . . When are you going back to England?'

'Monday or Tuesday.'

'Why can't you wait until the next weekend?'

'Because I've got to be back in England before I can give the police the registration letters of the car if they're not to have every chance of proving I broke the terms of bail and went abroad.'

'I'm coming with you.'

'No,' he said sharply.

'Why not?'

'Because it would make things ten times harder for me.'

'When life decides to kick you, it can really make a good job of things . . . All right. From now on, there's no future and for us there is only now. When we leave here we'll go to somewhere where we can forget that there is a rest of the world.'

He hesitated, then said: 'I want to return to the motel.'

'For God's sake, why?'

'I can't stop wondering if the Bressonaud woman booked in for the two of them but she was the only one who turned up.'

'What if she was?'

He answered wearily: 'I don't know. But it would be an odd thing to do without a reason.'

'And you think the manager will tell you anything?'

'He might be more helpful than he was last time.'

'Pigs might fly . . . Angus, we'll leave here and drive to somewhere very special. A little village called Persoul, in the St Amour foothills. I saw it the year before last and it was so lovely and the name of the hills was so appropriate that I promised myself that there's where I'd have my honeymoon.'

'We'll go there after the motel.'

'There won't be time,' she said sulkily.

'We won't be at the motel for long and afterwards I'll drive hard to make up the time.'

'Can't you understand, I don't want to go back to that place? I can't stop remembering that disgusting man with his periscope . . .'

'It'll be broad daylight and we won't be doing anything a maiden aunt couldn't watch. Hopefully, that part comes later.'

The proprietor came up to their table and greeted Belinda as a friend and asked if their meal had been to their satisfaction: he received their praise with a complacency that lacked any suggestion of modesty. He explained to Belinda how the sauce had been prepared, offered them a second liqueur, then moved on to the next table.

'Are you ready to move?' Sterne asked.

'No. I don't want to leave.'

'Because you're scared you'll be leaving happiness behind?'

'Damnit, you seem to be able to read my mind.'

He shook his head. 'It's just that we often think alike.'

CHAPTER 17

At the motel, the receptionist recognized them and immediately assumed they wanted a cabin for another night, but Belinda explained that they would like a word with the manager. The receptionist looked doubtful. The manager was very busy because head office had unexpectedly demanded an extra stocktaking . . . Belinda asked him if he would see if the manager could spare the time. He went into the small office and when he returned it was to say, with some surprise, that the manager would.

The manager had taken off his coat and was working in his shirtsleeves and obviously was very busy. The thought occurred to Sterne—but it was gone almost as soon as it had formed—that, remembering the other's previous hostility, it was perhaps strange that he should now agree to speak to them.

Belinda said, translating Sterne's questions: 'You told the police that the Bressonauds booked a double room?'

'All our cabins are double,' replied the manager, his manner brisk, watchful, but not overtly antagonistic.

'Did they both book in, or did one of them do it for the two?'

'I can't say. How can that matter?'

'It would confirm that only Madame Bressonaud was here.'

'Confirm? Who says that's the case?'

'The staff have told us there was no sign of her husband. Who actually did the booking in?'

'I've no idea . . .' began the manager, then stopped. He fidgeted with the plaited belt he wore round his trousers, finally said: 'I'll see if I can find out for you.' He came round the desk. 'Please have a seat.' He moved a chair closer to Belinda before hurrying out of the room and closing the door.

He was away some time and when he returned he was slightly breathless, as if he'd been hurrying. 'I'm sorry to have been so long, but the receptionist who was on duty at the time is now at home and I had to phone him there . . . He thinks Monsieur Bressonaud was with his wife, even though it was Madame Bressonaud who signed the register.'

'Wasn't that odd?'

'I don't understand.'

'Surely if a husband and wife stay here it's always the husband who books in?'

'In the old days, certainly. In these days . . . It is difficult to keep up with the changing customs.'

'Can the receptionist describe Monsieur Bressonaud?'

'I'm afraid not.'

'Why's that?'

'We have so many guests during the season . . .'

'But he must remember something about the husband if he thinks he was present.'

'His memory for particular details is a little hazy.'

'Then he could be mistaken and in fact Madame Bressonaud was alone?'

The manager hesitated. He cleared his throat. 'He thinks he was with his wife,' he said, repeating his previous words.

They thanked him briefly for his help, then left. As they crossed the foyer, Belinda said in a low voice: 'Well?'

'Was he genuinely trying to help, or just wanting to seem to be genuinely trying to help?' replied Sterne.

'What's the answer.'

'God knows. I don't.'

Once seated again behind the wheel, Sterne asked: 'Which way do we go from here?'

'The quickest is up to Perigueux and then across on the

main road: if we try a more direct route we'll end up on mountain tracks that are more for goats than cars.'

'How far is it to Persoul?'

'A long way.'

'Then we'll just keep going. Does your hotel have a night porter?'

'I don't know.'

'If necessary, we'll stop and phone ahead and find out. If it doesn't, we'll probably have to break off for the night.'

'I told you we shouldn't have come back here.'

He was about to point out that the time this had taken was unlikely to prove to have made that much difference, but a quick look showed her expression to be so strained that he said nothing. He drove out of the forecourt.

It was eight o'clock when he said: 'We're going to have to stay somewhere for the night.' He yawned.

'I suppose so,' she answered reluctantly.

'Otherwise, we'll get too tired. And in any case, we need a drink and a meal—though not much after that lunch—to recharge our batteries.'

They'd been climbing slowly but steadily for half an hour and the countryside had changed from lush pastures and fields heavy with corn to a stony soil which grew poor grass and stunted trees. Villages were few and far apart and those that they passed through had an air of decay, with houses with broken shutters and peeling paint.

'Have you any idea how far it is before we reach a place that's likely to have a reasonable hotel?' he asked.

'I'll check.' She reached for the map on the dashboard. 'We passed a fairly big town on our right not long ago.'

He looked briefly to his right. The land now fell away quite sharply and there was an extensive view, but his quick glance showed him no houses at all. In any case, there were few side roads and all those that he'd noticed had looked as if they might soon peter out in the yard of one of the subsistence-level farms. . . . He automatically checked the rear-view mirror. Some way behind them was a white car. Presumably, it was the same one that had been behind them some time back . . .

She said: 'Fauteville is something like twenty kilometres ahead and I seem to remember it's quite a big place.'

'Then we'll spend the night there and have a really early start in the morning.'

'Not too early.' She leaned sideways so that she could rest her head against the pillar of the car.

She was emotionally, rather than physically, exhausted, he thought. She had been right, they shouldn't have returned to the motel. They'd learned nothing, and for a reason that wasn't entirely clear to him, it had affected her deeply . . . Movement in the rear-view mirror attracted his attention. The white car—now identified as a big Peugeot—was immediately behind them. 'Why is it,' he asked rhetorically, 'that people will still climb up your exhaust pipe even when there's all the room in the world to pass?'

She said dreamily: 'The herd instinct.'

The Peugeot swung out to overtake them, then drew back in. Ahead of them, perhaps three-quarters of a kilometre away, was an oncoming lorry which, even at that distance, could be judged to be old, decrepit, and incapable of much speed. 'The bloke behind us needs L-plates up. He could have overtaken us and been half-way to the horizon before the lorry closes.'

'Not everyone can be as brilliant as you.'

This was the first time she'd shown signs of pulling out of her previous depression. His tone became light. 'Don't you mean anyone?'

'Big head!' She reached out and rested her fingers on his neck in the gesture of love with which he had become familiar.

The lorry passed them, rattling its way to some local farm. The Peugeot drew out, accelerated, and came abreast of them. It moved closer to crowd them.

'The driver's a bloody lunatic or blind drunk . . .' He caught sight of the look on the passenger's face and he realized with shocked and chilling certainty that the driver was neither insane nor drunk . . . He rammed the gear into third and floored the accelerator and the Renault surged forward, engine note soaring.

'What's the matter, Angus?'

The gap between the two cars widened for only a short while, then it began to close with an ever increasing speed. He judged that the Peugeot was turbo-charged, which meant there wasn't a chance of losing it with straight speed . . . Its bonnet drew level with the driving seat. On their right the land now dipped away sharply and to go over the edge would be disastrous . . . He tried to will more speed out of the Renault, but there was nothing left. He braked violently and fought the wheel, killing an incipient skid with opposite lock. The Peugeot surged ahead, crossing the path they would have taken if he hadn't braked.

'Are they bloody mad?' she demanded, her voice high.

'Just vindictive,' he answered grimly.

The Peugeot was faster and heavier. So in a straight slogging match they stood no chance and their only hope was to use guile to evade it until they reached a built-up area or the traffic increased and the driver would no longer dare to crash them.

The Peugeot's brake lights went on. He accelerated and swerved out and they passed. 'How far's it to the next village?'

She reached for the map and opened this out, found difficulty in reading it because of the motion of the car.

The Peugeot began to close the gap. He pulled over to the left-hand side of the road and took his foot off the accelerator and dabbed the brakes, then accelerated. The driver of the Peugeot, thinking Sterne was going to repeat his previous manœuvre, braked violently: before he could rectify his mistake, the gap between the two cars had become a couple of hundred metres.

'There's some sort of village about five kilometres on,' she said tautly. 'But it can't be much of a size.'

It didn't matter how small. The men in the Peugeot would not risk trying to kill them there.

The Peugeot was closing the gap. The driver knew he must either brake or accelerate and sooner or later—almost certainly sooner—the driver would judge correctly . . . He looked to his right. The land sloped as steeply as before and the rocks in the fields had become boulders . . .

The car momentarily jerked as the engine note changed pitch before resuming its shrill, frenzied rhythm—a warning that he was stressing it too highly and should slow . . .

A kilometre ahead, the road curved to the right and a heavy lorry appeared round the bed. The Peugeot had drawn almost abreast, but was not closing the gap between them. With the lorry in sight, the driver wasn't going to risk making a move. Since every second brought them closer to the village . . . Too late, he realized that they'd outmanœuvred him. He was still on the wrong side of the road so that if they matched his moves he'd be unable to draw in to the right, which meant he'd meet the oncoming lorry head on. He couldn't increase speed and they'd know he couldn't. So they'd be waiting for him to brake. And because the driver would be ready for this, his reaction time would be quick and, since the Peugeot was heavier and better braked, there was every chance he'd be able to prevent the Renault escaping . . .

'Look out, Angus,' Belinda shouted.

They were closing the lorry very quickly: it was a trailer

outfit, huge and heavy. To hit it would be like hitting a brick wall. The lorry flashed its lights.

The lorry's headlights were switched on to full beam and even above the scream of the Renault's engine they could hear the strident blast of its air horn. He braked, this time so violently that with opposite lock he only just managed to retain control. The Peugeot matched his move and came further into the centre of the road to cut off any chance of the Renault's being able to slide between it and the lorry.

Sterne's mind raced. By now, the lorry-driver would be convinced he was faced by a maniac and he'd try to get as far in to his side of the road as he could. How quick would his reactions be? Above normal, surely, since driving was his trade? Sterne drew further over to the left, apparently deliberately provoking the coming crash. Belinda screamed. The lorry-driver, frantically trying to avoid the catastrophe, steered to his left, so sharply that the trailer wrenched at its couplings. The Renault clipped the grass verge and the near-side front wheel bounced up as the lorry, a wall of buffeting air, came abreast of them. The trailer was snaking and threatening to whiplash them and Sterne had to steer back on to the verge. This time, the whole left-hand side of the car was thrown up into the air.

As they landed with a sickening jolt, the wheel was spun violently out of his hand. The end of the trailer drew clear as the tail of the Renault whipped round with a force that jerked their necks; their horizon became a blur as they spun across the road with tyres screaming. There was the ear-hurting screech of metal against metal as they slammed into the side of the Peugeot, then they were rolling.

The windscreen disintegrated, showering them with glass. Centrifugal forces left them incapable of movement or coherent thought. There was a violent jolt, one more roll, and they struck a boulder half the size of the car. He lost consciousness.

CHAPTER 18

There were formless mists as he became aware of himself. Then there was pain, at first remote, but all too soon immediate. Someone murmured meaningless but comforting words: the mists closed in and there was nothing.

Later there was form. A room with a high ceiling and a central light with a frilly, plastic shade which made him think of Brighton boarding-houses. He stared at the shade and tried to work out how he could have come to be faced by such a monstrosity, but the pounding pain in his head had made the problem too difficult. He closed his eyes and drifted off into an uneasy sleep that was filled with violent nightmares.

Someone was talking. He opened his eyes and saw a man and a woman, neither of whom he'd ever seen before. The man began to speak in English, slowly and very carefully. 'How do you do now?'

He went to sit up, but at the first movement there was an explosion inside his head.

'Be still and not wriggle.'

Wriggle was a bloody funny word to use. But the message was clear and if moving caused such agony, he was going to lie very still.

'How many of fingers?' asked the man as he held up three fingers in front of Sterne's face.

'Three,' he answered, in a croaky voice.

'Good.'

So what the hell was good about that?

'And now?'

'One.'

'Please to look.'

He watched the man's forefinger move from right to left. Perhaps he'd landed up in an asylum.

'Now you sleep.'

A woman came closer to the bedside. She was wearing a rather severe white uniform, but it was clear she was a very attractive blonde. Well formed, to boot.

She spoke in French and although he didn't understand every word he was fairly certain she'd said that his natural reflexes certainly appeared to be normal.

She injected something into his right buttock and before long he'd lost consciousness once more.

The door opened and Belinda entered. Her face looked worn and there were dark lines under her eyes: her left wrist was bandaged.

She crossed to the bedside, studied him for several seconds, then bent over until she could rest her cheek against his. 'Oh my God, my God!' He felt the wet of tears.

He gripped her. 'Relax. Didn't anyone ever tell you that it's very difficult to get rid of a bad penny?'

'When I saw you all crumpled up in an untidy mess I thought you were dead. I wanted to die as well.'

'Thank heavens you didn't do a Romeo or I'd have been honourably obliged to do a Juliet.'

'You damned fool,' she said and brushed his cheek with her lips. She settled on the edge of the bed. 'The doctor says you've had severe concussion but your skull's not cracked even though the roof of the car was forced in and it hit you so hard.'

'Nothing but rocks between my ears.' He touched her left arm, above the bandage. 'How badly hurt were you?'

'Me? It's nothing. Only a fool woman could survive a crash like that and then strain her wrist climbing out of the wreck.'

The door opened and a nurse looked into the room.

'It's all right, I'm just coming,' Belinda said in French.

The nurse closed the door.

'She didn't want me to come in and see you because you were so weak. I had to promise I wouldn't be in here for longer than a minute. I really must go now or she'll make an awful fuss next time.' She stood.

'In Spain,' he said, 'when anyone goes into hospital there's a second bed in the room for the relative or friend who helps look after the invalid.'

'I think it's probably a good job we're in France.' She kissed him and left.

He slept, woke, was given a light meal which was surprisingly tasty. By now his headache had eased to the point where he was becoming irked by being in bed. When Belinda came into the room he greeted her with much of his old energy.

She kissed him as he sat up in bed. 'You're looking a whole world better.'

'I'm feeling a whole world better.'

'Thank God for that . . . Angus, darling, the police want to talk to you. The doctor had a word with me about this and he said that the thing to do was to find out how you feel about things.'

'I'm going to have to see someone sooner or later, so I might as well make it sooner . . . Have they questioned you about the crash?'

'Later that first night. I told them the Peugeot tried to crowd us off the road and you tried desperately to get clear, but when the lorry came along in the opposite direction you couldn't do anything but go round the wrong side of it. I said the driver of the Peugeot must have been drunk . . . I reckoned that if I'd told them what really happened they'd have got in touch with the English police and then everything would have come out.'

'Clever as well as decorative!' His words were facetious, but his tone was serious. She must have been severely shocked, yet she'd had sufficient nous to realize the consequence of telling the truth.

'Angus . . . Why did those men in the car try to kill us?'

'I've been trying to work that one out and I'm damned if I've come up with an answer. On the face of things, it's because we were asking questions at the motel. But as we didn't learn a damn thing, I can't see that it can be that.'

'God, I was terrified!'

'And you weren't doing the driving.'

She gripped his hand tightly. After a moment she said: 'The policeman's waiting around now. Will you see him?'

She left the room, to return with a man not as tall as she, who had a tough but good-natured face, and who was dressed a shade too carefully to be smart. He introduced himself, very seriously, in French as Officer Raoux of the Police Judiciaire of the Sûreté Nationale. He wished Sterne a quick and complete convalescence. Then he sat down and began to put questions, leaving Belinda to translate.

Sterne answered carefully. They'd been driving along the road and the white Peugeot had started to overtake them, but instead of pulling right ahead it had come over as if it were determined to crash into them. He'd used brakes and accelerator to try to get clear. Then a heavy lorry had rounded the bend ahead and because they'd been on the wrong side of the road they'd been boxed in. The only way to escape a head-on crash had been to try to go round the near-side of the lorry. They'd hit the grass verge and bounced off that, missing the rear of the lorry's trailer, but spinning across the road to hit the Peugeot. After that, he wasn't at all clear what had happened.

Raoux fingered his chin as if he'd discovered a stray hair, missed when shaving. 'How was the Peugeot being driven when it kept crowding you? Was it weaving about the road?'

The lorry-driver would have been questioned and he must have testified that as far as he could judge the Peugeot had been driven smoothly but crazily. 'I don't think it was, no.'

'When it came level with you each time, it wasn't swerving this way and that?'

'No.'

'What sort of speed were you doing when you were trying to draw away?'

'There wasn't time to check.'

'But presumably you were travelling about as fast as the car would go?'

'Yes.'

'So you were doing, perhaps, between a hundred and forty and a hundred and fifty kilometres an hour. When a driver is drunk at that speed he is usually all over the road.'

Sterne made no comment.

'When did you first notice this Peugeot?'

'In the rear-view mirror, a few seconds before it came up to us.'

'You've no idea if it had been following you?'

'I'm pretty certain it hadn't. I check the rear-view mirror regularly, even on that kind of a road, and there was no sign of it until it was right behind us.'

'You must know it didn't stop after the accident. The lorry-driver says that when he last saw it, it was travelling very steadily at high speed. It doesn't seem as if the driver could have been drunk.' Raoux, watching Sterne's face, continued: 'Can you suggest a reason why someone might have deliberately tried to kill you?'

'No, no way. I'm just out here on holiday.'

Raoux turned. 'And you, Mademoiselle Backman—have you been able to think of a reason?'

'I'm sure there isn't one.'

'Then I have no more questions . . . Thank you for your help.' He stood. 'And may I wish you both a very speedy recovery.'

After he'd gone, Sterne said: 'I don't think he bought the idea that the driver was tight.'

'Maybe not right away. The only thing is, if he can't find any other explanation, he'll have to fall back on that one. Surely there must be people who can be as tight as ticks and yet drive in a straight line?'

'Could be, I suppose, but everyone I know ends up doing the wiggle-woggle . . . Still, let's hope you're right. In the meantime, I've got to start moving.'

'You're not going anywhere until the doctor says you're fit enough.'

'All I have now is a bit of a head . . .'

'Please, Angus, don't be stupid.'

'But it's Saturday already and . . .'

'It's Tuesday,' she corrected. 'You were unconscious for over twenty-four hours and then they kept you very well sedated.'

'Tuesday! Christ! Ralph will be going round the bend as he's not heard from me.'

'Then ring him and tell him what's happened. Or if you're not up to it, I'll speak to him.'

'I'd better do it. If he thinks someone else knows I'm travelling on his passport he'll put his head under a train . . . Can you organize a phone in here and explain I must get through to England?'

She kissed him, running her fingertips over his cheek. 'And after that I must go and do some shopping.' She kissed him again, then left.

A nurse carried a telephone into the room and plugged it into a wall socket. She said in French that if he told the hospital operator what number he wanted, it would be obtained for him. He lifted the receiver and gave the number of Parsonage Farm, repeated this twice more before the operator was satisfied she'd correctly understood him. The connection was made in less than a minute and the ringing note began. It continued. The operator broke in to ask him if he wanted to try another number. He gave Ralph's office number.

This time, the call was answered almost immediately. 'Prince, Hatley, and Shayborne,' said a woman with a plummy voice.

'Is Mr Sterne there?'

'One moment, please, while I see if he's in his office.'

A brief pause, a couple of clicks, and then Ralph said: 'Sterne speaking.'

'Sterne speaking.'

'Angus? Thank God you've phoned. We've been going frantic. How badly were you injured?'

'Just a bang on the head. It doesn't seem to have done any permanent damage. I'll soon be out of hospital.'

'Angela's been practically burying you.'

'Tell her from me that it's only the good who die young.' It was only as he finished speaking that he remembered something. 'How in the hell did you know I'd been in a car accident?'

'It was in the *Sunday Telegraph*.'

'It was what?' he said loudly, then regretted this because there was a sudden stab of pain in his head.

'There were just a couple of lines at the bottom of a page—I think they're called fillers. An English tourist, Ralph Sterne, had been in a car accident near Fauteville, in central France, and had been severely injured.'

'If Young or any of his blokes read the *Sunday Telegraph* rather than the *News of the World* . . .'

'Young was round before lunch on Sunday to find out if I was the injured Ralph Sterne. He demanded to know where you were and asked to see my passport.'

'What did you do?'

'I told him you were moving around the country and I didn't know exactly where, but if you got in touch with me I'd ask you to ring him.'

'And what did you do about the passport?'

'Told him of course he could see it. Went up to our bedroom, waited a bit, returned downstairs and apologized because Angela had been tidying up and changing things around and I didn't know where she'd put the passports for safety.'

'Did he believe you?'

'I . . . No, not really.'

'So he'll have contacted all ports and airports and warned them to look out for me, travelling on your passport?'

'I think you'd better reckon on that.'

If they caught him on entry, they'd arrest him for breaking bail and they'd charge Ralph with aiding and abetting—not forgetting the twenty thousand pounds which would be forfeited. If he stayed abroad and failed to turn up at the trial, they'd issue a warrant for his arrest . . . 'Ralph, we've still one chance. You've got to take the risk of giving Young the registration letters . . .'

'Angus, we've been through all that before, but you still don't seem to understand. Right now, whatever Young's suspicions, he can't be certain it was you in that car crash. After all, there are hundreds of other Ralph Sternes in the world and the one who crashed in central France just could have been one of them, I just could have mislaid my passport, and you just could be drifting around England using up the time until the trial. So to prove it was you would take time and work and he's told us that he can't ask a foreign force to undertake anything unless he can fully justify the request at the time it's made. At the moment he won't act,then. But if I give him the car registration letters it becomes obvious you've managed to find Belinda Backman which means it *was* you in that crash in France . . .'

'Not necessarily. When I told him about Belinda I said she'd promised to phone me if she decided she wanted to see me again. All right, she did and she's just phoned. I wasn't at home so you took the message and then asked her about the registration letters. She gave them to you.'

'And you think he'll swallow that? The first thing he'll do is demand that you identify yourself to someone in authority to prove you're still in this country.'

'Identify myself in person?'

'What the hell d'you think?'

'All right. Then I've just got to sneak back into the country without anyone knowing.'

'Impossible.'

'The impossible merely takes a little longer.'

'For God's sake, stop thinking everyone but yourself is a bloody fool. You'll be caught the moment you try to get in . . . Look, forget all that nonsense. Hang on where you are until the doctors are absolutely certain it's safe for you to move: don't rush back here for nothing, risking a relapse . . .'

'It's a risk I'm going to have to take,' cut in Sterne.

'Don't be so goddamn stupid,' said Ralph, exasperation making him angry. 'There's no way you can get back without being spotted.'

'Like to bet on that?'

'It's betting that started this whole mess off, isn't it?'

'Thanks very much for that timely reminder.'

'Angus, I was . . .' Ralph stopped abruptly. When he next spoke, his voice was flat in tone: 'I've told Angela what's happening. She can accept trouble so much better if she's forewarned about it.'

Sterne wondered how she'd received the news. Had she been bitter that things had gone so wrong? Almost certainly not, he decided. She was someone who could make a decision which involved risk and then, if the decision turned out to have been the wrong one, accept the consequences without bitter recriminations.

CHAPTER 19

There was a restaurant in the basement of the hospital. Belinda and Sterne sat at one of the corner tables. He finished a plate of trifle, flavoured with brandy and topped with whipped cream, looked across at her. 'Coffee?'

'Please. Black with a dash.'

He left the table and went over to the self-service counter, returning with two cups and saucers on a tray. He crossed to another, unoccupied table, for a bowl of sugar, then sat. She helped herself to sugar. 'Have you decided what to do when we leave here?' she asked.

'I have to try and get back into England so that Ralph's in the clear. That means returning via either the Channel Islands or Ireland. The immigration officials won't be so alert, even if they've been briefed. And from either place I can travel on without going through immigration again.'

'Surely the police will have thought of that possibility and countered it?'

'The detective-superintendent is a dogged man, but not overburdened with imagination.'

Her voice sharpened. 'You don't really believe that; you can't. A man doesn't reach high rank if he's a fool.'

'High rank often means conformity rather than initiative.'

'You must think up something better.'

'That's the best there is.'

'Then we drive back home and see if Jean can help.'

'How could he begin to?'

'Because . . . What do you make of him?'

'Make?'

'What kind of work did he do?'

He shook his head.

'I told you, I don't know either. All I do know is that he retired before he married Evelyn. But retired from what? To us he's always been kind, generous, loving, gentle . . . But sometimes, when something's happened which he doesn't like, or someone's rude or deliberately obstructive, there's a sudden suggestion about him of . . . of a tiger: as if he's all tensed violence. And he's wealthy, but where did all his money come from?'

'Where's this leading to?'

'That he may have unorthodox sources to call on. So that if anyone can help you, he can.'

'Maybe. But I'm not involving him. When people have been as welcoming as Evelyn and he, you don't repay them by involving them in some stinking trouble.'

She drank some coffee, replaced the cup on the saucer. 'Angus . . . He's already involved.'

'How the hell d'you mean?'

'The last time I phoned him I explained what had happened and asked if he could help . . . Please don't get too angry.'

They turned into the drive and L'Ile Blanche came into view: in the deepening shadows and the space of the park it was easy to visualize the house as an island.

Evelyn and de Matour hurried out of the house and there was an emotional reunion. Again and again, Evelyn demanded to know if they were both really all right.

In the family sitting-room, they drank a bottle of welcome-home champagne, after which Belinda stood and said she was going upstairs for a long, hot, scented bath. Evelyn turned to Sterne. 'You'll want to do the same . . . you're in the red bedroom again, so the bathroom next door is all yours. There are towels and . . .'

'The domestic details can wait,' said de Matour, 'as can the bath until Angus and I have had a little discussion. To help us along with this, we will open—and perhaps consume—a second bottle of champagne.'

Evelyn looked quickly at her husband, then nodded. 'All right. And I'll see dinner's coming along smoothly and that Cécile hasn't let the foul mood she's been in all day ruin the coq au vin.'

After Evelyn and Belinda had left, de Matour opened a second bottle of champagne and refilled Sterne's and his own glass. He returned to his chair. 'Belinda told me over the telephone that you had a difficulty and would like some help?' His tone wasn't hostile, but it was reserved.

'She spoke to you without any reference to me: if I'd known what she intended to do, I'd have stopped her.'

'Would it not, perhaps, be more accurate to say you would have tried to stop her? She is a woman of decided character . . . Why would you have tried to stop her asking me for help? When she was in trouble, you helped her.'

'My trouble is a filthy mess.'

'Rape also is not pleasant.'

'I didn't run any risks. Anyone helping me could.'

'Is it not for such person, rather than you, to judge whether to accept that risk?'

'I'm not involving you,' said Sterne stubbornly.

'As to that . . . Will you tell me one thing? Did you not suspect that you were carrying drugs in the Mercedes?'

The expression on de Matour's face—in particular in his eyes—was hard. Sterne was abruptly reminded of Belinda's description of tensed violence. 'The money seemed a lot for just driving back to England so at the beginning I did reckon someone might be trying to take me for a sucker. So I had the car searched in Cala Survas by a mechanic who found nothing. This made me think I was being paid the extra solely to compensate for the risk of being picked up with false papers. Like a fool, I never imagined that anything might be planted on the car in Lençon.'

'If you were guilty of anything, then, it was of naivety.' De Matour drank. His expression relaxed and returned to its normal state of good humour. 'As an old man with too much experience, I have great sympathy for naivety. Therefore, I shall help you.'

'There's nothing you can do.'

'How can you be quite so certain?'

'I've only one hope and that's to try and make it back via the Channel Islands or Ireland, hoping the immigration officers won't be as wide awake as on the mainland.'

'You think that is possible? Or have you said that to Belinda in order to try and calm her fears?'

'Perhaps. And my own.'

De Matour chuckled, which seemed an odd thing to do at such a moment. He stood, went over to the champagne bottle, withdrew it from the ice bucket, carefully wrapped a napkin around it, and refilled Sterne's glass, even though Sterne had drunk only a couple of mouthfuls. 'Tell me, Angus, how well do you understand the official mind?'

'I'm not quite certain what you mean.'

'Have you had often to deal with the bureaucrats who govern—or try to—one's life in every civilized country, and most uncivilized ones as well?'

'No more often than's been absolutely necessary.'

'A very sensible attitude to adopt . . . I, on the other hand, once had to have a great deal to do with them. But perhaps Belinda has told you this?'

'Not really, no.'

De Matour chuckled. 'She's convinced that at one time

I was a pirate and I have no intention of disillusioning her. A woman will respect a man only when she loves him a lot or fears him a little . . . When I started work, I put all my money into a partnership and after a couple of years my partner disappeared, having swindled me out of everything because I'd trusted him implicitly. This taught me something which throughout my subsequent business career has been of the greatest possible value: you can make money or you can remain honest, but you cannot do both together. I started afresh and soon made a great deal of money. Eventually, because of my success, I was approached by the government of the day and asked if I'd investigate the country's public sector with a view to suggesting ways of improving its standards of efficiency. I discovered two things. First, that the public sector was an even greater morass of inefficiency than I had imagined: secondly, that although I could make recommendations which if implemented might introduce a degree of efficiency, such proposals would engender tremendous resentment and in any case would never actually come into effect because of bureaucracy's inbuilt tendency to inertia. Do you see where all this is leading?'

'Not really. I'm probably being very slow on the uptake.'

'I will explain more particularly. You are here and you need to be there, in England, but it is essential that no official can ever prove that you have been here or have travelled there. Now, how will the British Authorities expect you to try to return to England?'

'By smuggling myself in in a yacht, but that would take a lot of organizing and time's short, or entering through normal channels, chosing a port or airport where the immigration officials will not be very alert.'

'In other words, relying on their incompetence? Then remember that, despite popular belief, few bureaucrats are totally incompetent . . . So let us examine the problem from their view-point. How will they set about alerting staff at ports and airports to watch out for you?'

'They'll draw up a description of me and add to that a copy of my passport photo and the number of Ralph's passport.'

'What will they do with this information?'

The question seemed so unnecessary that Sterne replied impatiently. 'Make certain the men at the immigration desks have it.'

'Be more precise. The men at which desks?'

'The ones at which the passengers have to show their passports on arrival.'

'But these days, at the major points of entry, there are three—one for the British, the gentlemen, one for members of the Common Market, the players, and one for foreigners, the uninformed spectators. Will the details concerning you be sent to all three immigration desks at each port of entry?'

'No, of course not. They'll only go to the British one.'

'Why?'

'Because I'm British.'

'Exactly. An official mind knows that a British national must hold a British passport and so will always pass through the immigration control for Britons, even if travelling on another's passport. Therefore, to provide the other two desks with this information would be a waste of time and effort and the official mind never wastes his own time and effort, merely other persons' . . . So your way into the UK is obvious. You appear at the desk for Common Market citizens since there the official list of undesirables will be restricted to Marxists, assassins, and French politicians.'

'That's a non-starter. If I try that and show a British passport, I'll immediately be sent over to the British desk where I'll be scrutinized twice as thoroughly.'

De Matour laughed complacently. 'You have missed the point.'

'Which is what?'

'You do not present a British passport, but a French temporary travel permit.'

'And how in hell do I get my hands on one of those?'

'I will provide it.' Seeing Sterne's look of amazement, de Matour laughed with sly pleasure. 'As I mentioned a moment ago, I was once in a position to recommend fundamental changes in the structure, level of manning, and day-to-day working practice of a great number of bureaucratic institutions. While these recommendations, if made, would eventually have been suffocated, they must in the meantime inevitably have opened up many a Pandora's box. I took the opportunity of pointing this out to many of those most intimately concerned and each one of these persons was quick to argue the practical advantages of keeping the lids of those boxes shut and locked. I listened and eventually allowed myself to be won over by their eloquence. Naturally, one good turn deserves another and men of honour must always recognize their debts. So you will understand, if I now have a word with someone about providing you with a travel permit there will be no difficulties.'

'You mean you're going to . . .' Sterne cut short the words, recognizing that there were times when it was best not to go into details. 'But that's a hell of a risk. What happens to you if I'm caught?'

'There's not the slightest chance of that. The course of the official mind can be relied upon under all circumstances.'

'The immigration officer might start speaking French to me to find out how long I intend to stay in Britain.'

'No Frenchman would ever be able to understand an English official's fractured French.'

'It's a crazy idea.'

'Excellent. Nothing is better guaranteed to ensure its success.'

Sterne left the walkaway and carried on down the last stretch of corridor to immigration control. There was a long queue at the British desk, much shorter ones at the other two. He ran his forefinger around the top of his lightly coloured turtle-neck leisure shirt which Belinda had insisted he buy in Chinon because it was so chic, so French, and in England the kind of thing worn only by foreigners and homos . . .

The immigration officer was asking a woman a multitude of questions. It would, Sterne thought, be just his luck to meet some inquisitive bastard who spoke half a dozen languages fluently . . . The queue moved forward. And now, as if to make up for lost time, the immigration officer did little more than briefly study each newcomer, flick through the passport, look back and wave the person on. Soon, Sterne stood in front of the desk. He hoped the sweat on his forehead and neck wasn't yet obvious. The immigration officer examined the travel permit: his expression could have been disapproving, as if only second-class citizens were content with travel permits rather than passports. He looked back at Sterne. He handed the permit back and concentrated on the next man in the queue.

Sterne walked towards the luggage hall. He needed a drink, a very large drink, but he couldn't remember whether the ridiculous licensing laws applied to international airports.

CHAPTER 20

Sterne pushed his way through the crowd of waiting relatives and friends and crossed to a telephone kiosk. He checked the telephone directory for the number of a local car hire firm, rang them, and asked for a Fiesta to be delivered at the airport immediately. The woman he spoke to promised it would be in the short-term car park within twenty minutes. He dialled Parsonage Farm: Ralph answered. 'The prodigal brother has returned so cast an eye for a fatted calf.'

Ralph, his voice high, said: 'You mean . . . you're here? And you're not in custody?'

'Didn't I say there'd be no problem? I've been thinking things over and it'll look better if your passport and I don't suddenly appear at the same time in the same place. I'll stay with Leila and Andy, who live pretty close to here, then, once you've got your passport, you can ring Young and tell him the Rover's registration letters. So how about meeting at Spironi in an hour's time for a meal and the official passport handing-over ceremony?'

The restaurant was half a mile back from the A20 and before the motorway had opened it had been a popular stopping place for travellers: now, it was often virtually empty during the week. As he sipped a gin and tonic, Sterne stared at the large mural on the far wall and wondered if the Mediterranean scene had ever been so dazzlingly blue, white, and green, as the artist had made it . . .

Ralph entered, saw him, and hurried across. 'How are you, really?'

'Ninety-nine per cent recovered.'

'Thank God for that. When we read the news about the crash we were worried so sick we couldn't think straight.' He put his right hand on Sterne's arm as if to reassure himself, then quickly dropped it away, perhaps slightly embarrassed at having openly shown such emotion.

They sat. Sterne called a waiter over and ordered a whisky and a gin and tonic. Ralph, not fully aware of what he was doing, picked out a slice of crusty French bread from the wicker basket on the table and began to tease it with his fingers. 'How in hell did you manage to get back into the country without being caught?' He'd lowered his voice, even though the two nearest tables were unoccupied.

'I used a forged French temporary travel permit in the name of Robert Brousse.'

'My God! I wish I hadn't asked . . . It really was . . . forged?'

'Expertly.'

'If you'd been caught with a forged document on top of everything else . . .'

The waiter returned with the drinks.

When he had left and was out of earshot, Ralph said: 'How did the crash happen? Did you have a blowout?'

'Nothing like that. A large Peugeot worked it.'

'You mean, it wasn't an accident?'

'No way.'

'Christ! . . . Why should anyone have tried to kill you?'

'I wish I knew the answer. Belinda and I had been asking questions at the motel in Lençon, but we'd learned nothing and since there wasn't anything more we could do we decided to spend the last few days in the mountains, in a little village she knew. We were on our way when the Peugeot came up behind us and tried first to swipe us off the road, then to steer us into an oncoming lorry.'

'You must have discovered something dangerous to them.'

'Obviously they thought we had. But if they'd bothered to check with me first, I could have told them how mistaken they were.'

The waiter returned and served Ralph with another whisky.

Sterne said: 'Phone Young as soon as you get back and tell him the possible registration combinations are A one BDB to A nine nine nine BDB, and the car's a dark blue Rover: I can't say which model.'

'He'll start shouting for you.'

'Tell him I'm due to ring you very soon and you'll ask me to get in touch with him.'

Ralph nodded, lifted his glass, and drank.

The red Metro turned into the drive of Parsonage Farm and came to a stop by the side of the double garage. Young climbed out and stared at the house, and thought that though life had taught him the futility of dreaming, nothing could stop him dreaming of one day owning a house like this, a private piece of history, set in the quiet countryside . . . Meacher, beside him, said: 'I wonder what they find to do, living out here in the middle of nowhere?'

'Let's move,' Young said, annoyed to discover yet again how wide a gulf could exist between people.

Ralph opened the front door to them and he shook hands with punctilious good manners. He led the way into the sitting-room. 'I decided it was best to telephone you the moment I found the passport.'

Young said nothing.

'It had somehow dropped into a file so it was only when I opened the file for some papers that I found it.'

'I'd like to look at it, if you don't mind.' Young's tone was carefully neutral.

'Of course not. As a matter of fact, I've got it on me now.' Ralph brought the passport out of his coat pocket and handed it across.

Young opened the passport, checked through the pages, closed it. 'It's a pity immigration controls have given up stamping these,' he said as he handed it back. 'They used to help keep memories alive.'

'My wife would agree with you; she's a great person for memories,' replied Ralph blandly. 'By the way, when my brother phoned me, I told him you wanted to hear from him.'

'He got on to me late last night.'

'Then now you're satisfied that your suspicions were entirely wrong?'

'Not yet.'

'Why not?'

'Just routine. The phone call could have come from abroad so I've asked your brother to go to his nearest police station to identify himself. Until he's done that, I can't officially be satisfied that he is still in this country.'

'But unofficially?'

'Unofficially, I'm quite certain . . .' Young stopped himself.

'Now the business is over, have a drink?'

'Thank you, but we have to get back to work.'

Once they were seated in the Metro, Meacher said: 'Well?'

'How the bloody hell did he manage to slip back into this country?'

'By yacht? Port officials aren't always as wide awake as they might be.'

'You know as well as I do that for an amateur that's a sight easier talked about than done. And we had a general alert out to all coastguards.'

'Then have you got it all wrong and the Ralph Sterne in the car crash was nothing to do with here?'

'It was Angus Sterne, travelling on his brother's passport.'

'Well, he can't have come through the normal channels so that just leaves one answer. He was telephoning from France, hoping you'd buy his story that he was in Sussex.'

'What's the point of that if he can't go to a police station and identify himself.'

'He was hoping you wouldn't demand he did. But you did, so he's lost out. But he's not worried. He's shacked up with a woman and he's forgotten that there's a tomorrow.'

'Don't you ever lift your mind above sex?'

'Not unless I absolutely have to.'

The police station was an old building, part of a complex which had been added to from time to time and now was an architect's nightmare. The front room was square, shabby, and smelled of boiled cabbage and boot polish. The duty sergeant, an elderly, disgruntled man, studied Sterne. 'You say a Detective-Superintendent Young of the Kent police asked you to go to the nearest police station to identify yourself?'

'That's right.'

'It's the first I've heard of it.' He sighed. 'All right. Have you got a driving licence, credit card, anything of that nature?'

Sterne brought a wallet out of his breast pocket. 'Driving licence, Access and cheque cards.' He placed the things on the counter.

The sergeant examined them and compared the three signatures, then reached for a sheet of plain paper and a ballpoint pen. 'If you'll sign your name three times, making the same signature as on the cards.'

Sterne signed his name three times. The sergeant compared those signatures with the ones on the licence and cards, wrote a few notes on the bottom of the sheet of paper, turned the paper over so that there was no chance of Sterne reading what he'd written. 'That's all, then, Mr Sterne.'

'You'll get in touch with Superintendent Young?'

'That's right.'

Sterne telephoned Fording Cross divisional HQ several times the following morning and finally managed to speak to Young. 'Did the police at West Treshurst get in touch with you?'

'Yes.'

'So everything's cleared up?'

'I suppose you could put it like that.'

'Have you done anything about the registration numbers?'

'Swansea gave me four names and addresses and the four persons concerned have been interviewed.'

'With what result?' Sterne asked, his voice sharp from tension.

'None of them, or their cars, was in France on the relevant date.'

'One of them was. Someone's lying. You've got to go back and find out who.'

'Mr Sterne, the four men live in different parts of the country so were questioned by officers from four different county forces. Each of those officers was satisfied that he was being told the truth. On the facts available, the police are unable to take the matter further.'

'Don't you believe Belinda?'

'She could have made a mistake.'

'She didn't.'

'Letters can easily be misread at a distance, especially when seen only briefly.'

'What is it? You want me to be found guilty to prove what a clever detective you are? All right, you won't do anything. So give me the names and addresses and I'll find out who's lying.'

'That's quite out of the question.'

'Why?'

'Surely it's obvious that any investigation must be carried out by the police and not by an individual?'

'And when the police refuse to do anything?'

'I have explained the situation.' Young said a curt goodbye and cut the connection.

Sterne's thought's were both angry and bewildered. A man was innocent until proved guilty but it seemed that sometimes he would be prevented from establishing the facts which would deny such proof . . . He dialled Ralph's office. 'I've just spoken to the Detective-Superintendent. He's identified four possible Rovers and each of the owners has been questioned. They all deny being in France. But one of 'em's lying.'

'Angus, if the police have questioned them and are satisfied . . .'

'One of 'em must have bloody well been lying but Young refuses to have 'em questioned again. Get on to him and make him.'

'I can't.'

'What the hell d'you mean, you can't?'

'The way in which an officer conducts a case is within his own jurisdiction and it can only be questioned—in court—if it can be shown beyond any shadow of doubt that he's been negligent or guilty of malfeasance.'

'So he's been guilty of malfeasance—he won't check up again.'

'If he genuinely believes nothing's to be gained from further inquiries—and the burden of rebutting this assumption is entirely on the person who asserts he does not genuinely believe—then his judgement cannot be challenged.'

'God Almighty! A hundred words to say they've covered themselves in all directions.'

'It's not really like that at all. If only you'd look at things reasonably . . .'

'How the hell can I? I'm the poor sod who's got his

goolies caught in the nut-crackers . . . If he won't question the four again, I will.'

'That's quite out of the question.'

'Why?'

'The private individual's never entitled to take the law into his own hands—subject to a couple of minor exceptions. On top of that, you are out on bail . . .'

'Can you get hold of the names and addresses for me?'

'The Superintendent certainly won't give them to me.'

'Why can't you get on to Swansea? From time to time, solicitors must need to know in civil cases who the owners of cars are.'

'Yes, but . . . but even if I did obtain the names, what could you possibly hope to do?'

'Come face to face with each of the four and find out which one of 'em was in that Rover on the outskirts of Vertagne.'

'You can't . . . Angus, you told me they deliberately tried to kill you in France.'

'Well?'

'Then they're obviously very dangerous. If you should personally identify the driver of the Rover he could try a second time to kill you. It would be insane to run the risk. You've got to leave the police to handle things.'

'I would, if they hadn't refused.'

'But . . .' Ralph became silent. As a lawyer, he believed both in the sanctity of innocence and the certainty that when such innocence was challenged its defence must be left to the legitimate forces of justice. But how did one square those two beliefs when the forces of justice refused to act . . .

He made one last effort to change his brother's mind. 'You'll be risking everything for nothing. I've told you, even if you identify one or more of the men behind the smuggling, that won't prove you innocent of the charge of knowingly smuggling in the heroin.'

'Maybe,' replied Sterne harshly, 'but it wasn't just me they tried to murder in France. It was Belinda as well.'

Of the four names Ralph had given Sterne, one man lived in Crawley, one in Olningham, one in Manchester, and the fourth in Haddington. Crawley being the nearest town, he drove there and spoke to the self-satisfied, patronizing owner of an up-market antique shop: this man resembled neither of the two in the Rover in Vertagne. Sterne left Crawley and, after spending one night with friends en route, continued on to Suffolk.

The river Olner had been of considerable importance in mediaeval times and Olningham had been a busy port, but then the wide estuary had begun to silt up due to an unexplained change in the currents around that stretch of the coast and its importance had declined until only a handful of inshore fishing boats sailed from it. Then, after the turn of the present century, its popularity had gradually returned with the spread of yachting—mud flats now covered much of the mile and a half wide estuary, but there were two broad, if relatively shallow, channels of clear water and these allowed weekend yachtsmen to sail without ever risking the challenge of the open sea.

He reached the hotel, in Flood Street, in time for a mediocre dinner. Afterwards, he left and walked down Flood Street to Harbour Walk, in search of the owner of the second of the dark blue Rovers whose numbers Ralph had obtained from Swansea. The tide was now on the turn and beginning to ebb and ripples were forming on the upstream side of buoys. A hundred yards along a man was changing the plug of a moped and Sterne asked him where Bailey and Sons were. The man said round the corner.

There was a ship's chandler, its single display window filled with coils of rope and wire, chains, cleats, winches, and a pair of crossed kedge anchors, and then the road curved round to the left. Beyond was a two-hundred-yard stretch of wasteland, littered with rubbish, and the boat-yard, surrounded by a high chainlink fence. There were two sheds close together, one much larger than the other, several cradles, a slipway, a self-propelled hoist over a wet berth, and a quay. On the gabled end of the larger shed was a weathered board on which, in peeling paint, was the name BA LEY & S S.

Roughly in the middle of the chainlink fencing were two gateways, one for vehicles and the other for pedestrians. The single wooden door was half open. He went inside. What more natural than that a weekend visitor should rubberneck round?

He passed two motor-boats in cradles, one with a damaged hull below the waterline, the other with both screws removed, to come level with the smaller of the two sheds. Looking beyond this, he saw a concrete apron and the quay; several craft were tied up and the slight wind was keeping the halyards tapping against masts to provide the background sounds heard wherever there were boats. He continued past the shed to the quayside. There were a couple of fast-looking powerboats, an open, cathedral-hull boat with an enormous outboard that was weighing down her stern, a couple of tidy yachts, a ketch with elaborate upperworks, a trawler yacht . . . His gaze came back to the trawler yacht as he studied her lines more closely. Sharply raked bows, a wheelhouse with for'd inclined ports, a look-out point above the wheelhouse shaped like a stumpy funnel, a mast with boom, made to look top-heavy by an enclosed radar scanner . . . There was something familiar about her. He walked along the quay. He noticed above the wheelhouse an elegantly shaped trumpet foghorn and now he was certain he'd seen her before . . . He continued on until he could read her name on the stern. *Morag III*, registered in Olningham.

He'd once known a smiling, elfin Morag who'd taught him that when young the only true meaning of life was enjoyment . . . He remembered. *Morag III* had been in the harbour at Cala Survas.

It was too much of a coincidence to be meaningless, yet what it meant he couldn't begin to judge beyond the fact that someone connected with the boatyard had surely been driving that dark blue Rover in Vertagne . . .

'What the bloody hell d'you think you're doing?'

He turned. A short, stumpy man, with leathered complexion, dressed in a roll-neck sweater despite the warmth, and paint-splashed jeans, had come round the corner of the larger shed. 'Just looking at the boats,' he answered.

'You ain't no right here.'

'The road gate was open so I didn't think it would do any harm to have a look.'

'It were shut.'

'It wasn't,' corrected Sterne, with continuing good humour. 'If it had been, I wouldn't have come in.'

The man scratched his wiry hair. 'It should've been shut.'

'No harm done, I hope. I always take the chance to look at boats, especially those made for going to sea rather than harbour-drinking.' He pointed at the trawler yacht. 'She looks as if she'd cross over to the Continent without much trouble.'

The man said scornfully: 'She's built for going near anywhere you like to think of.'

'Could she go as far as the Mediterranean?'

'Yeah.'

'Has she been down there?'

'What's it to you?'

Sterne shrugged his shoulders. 'It's just that I've a friend who's in the charter trade in the Med and he says that the market for the big, luxury yacht is getting very sticky and people want the smaller boats. Does she belong to a local man?'

'Ain't no business of yours who she belongs to, is it?'

'No, of course not.'

'Then stop being so bloody inquisitive and get out of here.'

They walked in silence along the quay to the smaller shed where they turned left. They were in time to see someone come out of the far end of the shed.

'So that's why the door was bloody open,' muttered the man by Sterne's side. 'Always on at everyone else to keep things tight shut . . .' He raised his voice to a shout. 'You left the outside gate open.'

'What was that?'

'Always bloody deaf when it suits him . . . I said, you left the outside gate open.'

They closed until they could see each other clearly, despite the rapidly failing light. Sterne recognized the driver of the blue Rover at the same moment as he was recognized.

CHAPTER 21

Sterne took a pace forward.

'Stop him.'

Sterne began to run. He'd taken no more than a couple of steps when his right leg was expertly hooked and he crashed to the ground with a force that jarred the whole of his body. As he struggled to recover from the crash, he heard them talking.

'It's Sterne. Where'd he come from?'

'All I bloody know is, I found him wandering around, looking at the boats, because you left the bloody gate open . . .'

'Get him into the office.'

The first man had drawn a knife from a sheath and he brought this down so that the tip pricked Sterne's neck. 'Move.'

Sterne dragged himself to his feet. A hand tightened on his right arm and twisted him round until he was facing a door halfway up the side of the larger shed. 'In there.'

The door was locked. The second man went forward, unlocked the door, and switched on some lights. Sterne was pushed inside. The main floor space was taken up by two motor-cruisers under construction. They continued past both of them to come to a set of offices, partitioned off with wood and glass. They entered the first one. Sterne was forced down into a chair.

The second man settled on the edge of the desk. He said abruptly: 'What have you told the police to get them asking questions? How d'you know to come here?'

Sterne tried to sound bewildered. 'What are you talking about? What d'you think you're doing . . .' He gasped as he was suddenly kicked in the ankle with a steel-protected industrial boot. He started to reach down to try to rub away some of the shooting pain and a fist slammed into the side of his neck, almost knocking him from the chair.

'We'll need help.' The second man turned and lifted up the telephone receiver, dialled. 'It's Steve. Get down to the office and bring Joe . . . Yeah, trouble, but nothing we can't handle.' He replaced the receiver.

'If you hadn't left the bloody outside gates open . . .' began the first man.

'You think he'd have just gone away? What happened when you found him?'

'I told you. Said he'd just wandered in to look at the boats, being keen on 'em. I wasn't bloody well to know . . .'

'Did he seem interested in any particular boat?'

'He wanted to talk about *Morag*.'

'That figures.' The second man stared across at Sterne, his strongly featured face half in shadow. 'It's a pity they made a right balls-up of getting you in France.'

The first man said: 'You mean it's him—the same bloody bloke?'

'Well, it isn't Prince Charlie.'

'And it's because of him the police was asking about the car? How'd he know?'

'That's what we've got to find out.' He turned to Sterne. 'Where's the woman?'

'What woman? What are you talking about?'

Unseen by Sterne, the second man must have given a signal. A boot slammed into his ankle for the second time and he cried out from the scalding pain.

'Did you get the number of the car when you were stopped in the village?'

'What village?'

A horn sounded twice. 'Watch him,' said the second man. 'I'll let 'em in.' He stood, came round the desk and left the office.

Sterne acknowledged that when the two newcomers were present, he wouldn't have a ghost of a chance. They'd torture him into telling them all that had happened and then they'd kill him. And with the sea half an hour's sailing down the estuary, there wouldn't be any problem over getting rid of his body. So his only chance of escape was now, while there was just the one man guarding him . . . He groaned, reached down to his ankle and massaged it. 'It's broken,' he said, making his voice thin and scared.

The man sniggered.

The chair had arms and he took a grip on these and lifted himself up to ease his right foot off the ground. He heard the movement but didn't take any avoiding action and the blow caught him flush in the neck. He fell sideways, making it seem the force had been greater than it had, and deliberately went over with the chair to crash to the floor.

'Bloody get up.'

Very slowly, he came to a kneeling position.

'Right up, you stupid bastard.'

'My ankle's broken.' From outside, he heard a dull thump which he translated as the sound made by the closing of the outside gates.

The man jerked the chair up on to its legs. He moved the knife until its point pierced Sterne's lightweight jacket and shirt to prick his stomach. 'Into the chair.'

Sterne reached up to the arms of the chair for support, laboriously heaved himself up, keeping his right leg lifted as if he could not bear the slightest weight on it. The man, contemptuous of a cripple, had lowered the knife and come round the chair until he was on Sterne's right-hand side. Sterne lashed out with his right foot and landed the toe in the man's crotch. He staggered back, instinctively clutching himself with his free hand to meet the inevitable agony. He tried to straighten up to use the knife, but couldn't.

Sterne ran out of the office and past the boats. He heard a car come to a stop: the engine was cut. He reached the outside door and pulled it open. The car was parked a hundred feet away, just beyond the sheds, and three men had begun to walk away from it. He ran towards the river. There was a shout and feet began to pound on the concrete path.

He reached the end of the shed, came out on to the concrete apron and quay, turned right. When he drew level with the far corner of the shed, he judged that the chainlink fencing was two hundred yards away. Scattered haphazardly between him and the fence were several boats which were clearly hulks, abandoned as being beyond economic repair. These offered some cover now that it was almost dark. He dropped into the shadow of a motor-boat on its side.

There was a shout. 'Switch the lights on.'

Outside lights could mean arc lamps which would illuminate everywhere. Then, this hulk could cease to be a hiding-place but would become a trap. He had to make the chainlink fence before the lights came on. How high was it? Memory suggested somewhere between eight and ten feet: memory also added a two-strand barbed wire top which jutted outwards to prevent easy ingress. Even assuming the links were large enough to give him footholds, the barbed wire would, at the very least, slow him right down . . . He heard sounds of running beyond him, probably by the fence. The sounds stopped. One of the men, waiting for any sounds which would suggest that the fence was being climbed? Because the climb must be a slow and difficult one, it was virtually inevitable that he'd be caught before completing it . . . He couldn't go forward. So he had to turn back . . .

He remembered the boats. He left the cover of the hull and moved slowly, despite the need for speed, because if he were to be successful he had to move unnoted. He reached the quay and heard the constant chuckle of the water, now ebbing strongly. Satisfied he dared move more quickly, he continued until he came abreast of the first of the boats tied up . . . Arc lights came on, leaving him totally exposed. He waited for the first shouts, but there was none. Because they'd known in which direction he'd first fled, they'd correctly assumed he'd been making for the perimeter fence and were concentrating on that side. But it wouldn't take them any time to realize that he must have doubled back . . .

He was abeam of a motor-boat. Astern of her was *Morag III*, now noticeably lower in relation to the quay. He went along and climbed aboard and as he did so his foot caught on something which trailed across the deck and rapped a stanchion.

'What was that?' someone shouted.

He reached the outside door of the wheelhouse and found this locked, but someone had carelessly left a port partially open. By standing on tiptoe and twisting sideways, he was just able to get his arm inside and reach down far enough to lower the port all the way. He climbed inside. The engine controls were for'd, on the port side, set in a single panel: because most of the controls and dials were duplicated, it was clear that she was twin-engined. The keys were not in the switches.

A couple of years before he'd done a good turn for a man who, by way of thanks, had shown him how to bypass a car's ignition switch—an accomplishment which until now he'd had no occasion to make use of. He checked and found the panel which gave access to the back of the control board and then, by touch, identified the wires leading to the nearer, starboard, switch. There was slack on the wires and this enabled him to wrench them free and bring out the ends. He looked through the nearest port. A man came into sight from beyond the far shed and visually checked the line of boats, shouted something that was too muffled to be understood, then returned the way he'd come and disappeared.

The after door of the wheelhouse was in two halves, one secured solely by the lock, the other by bolts made fast top and bottom. After sliding these bolts undone, Sterne was able to pull the doors inboard until the tongue of the lock sprang free and both of them could be clipped fully open. He went aft and let go the stern line. Immediately, the stern was caught by the tide and began to sheer out from the quay. He went for'd and took two turns off the head rope, then, leaving a final turn round the cleat, made for the wheelhouse, carrying the line with him and careful to keep it under tension. He made the line fast round the corner of the wheelhouse, using the port and the doorway. Now, he could let go for'd by releasing the rope from the wheelhouse.

The man—he presumed he was the same one—came back round the end of the shed and now he had a torch. He shone the beam on to the first craft and was slowly sweeping the beam aft when his attention was caught by the trawler yacht, her stern well out into the river. He shouted.

Sterne coupled up the wires and got the wrong combination the first time: the second time, the starter engaged and the engine fired. He put on starboard helm, advanced the throttle. There were low-pitched, intermittent creaks from the rope as it took more strain. He went aft and, judging the moment, released the rope: it snaked out of the wheelhouse, across the deck, and into the water. The combination of tide, helm, and single screw, brought her round quickly until she was heading down-river.

The beam of the torch caught and held the wheelhouse, but now there was a gap of twenty yards between the quay and the boat. He advanced the throttle and put on helm to counteract the turning action of the single screw. He again looked across at the boatyard, rapidly falling astern, and suddenly realized he'd been congratulating himself too soon.

Men were scrambling down into one of the powerboats.

CHAPTER 22

The arithmetic of any pursuit was obvious. Forgetting the tide—it would affect both boats—he could make perhaps ten knots on the one engine while the speedboat was possibly capable of forty. But there was more to it than just speed. The speedboat was a relatively frail craft, while the trawler yacht was strongly built for the open seas: physical contact would be far more dangerous to them. So if he were skilful enough, he could keep them at bay until he reached the mouth of the estuary and the open sea and then, unless it was flat calm, they'd never be able to keep up with him.

He looked back again. Two men were climbing down into the second speedboat. So it was going to be two, not one, against him . . . A fierce bellow of sound showed that the engine of the first boat had been started . . .

When he reached the bifurcation of the river and turned into the right-hand channel, marked by flashing buoys, he could just make out a bow wave aft. It closed rapidly. Then the note of the speedboat's engine changed pitch and he judged they were slowing in order to match his speed. He waited until they were almost abeam, altered course sharply. The bows came round until they were on a collision course. For a moment it seemed the speedboat was not going to give way, then it abruptly sheered off. He grinned. They'd got the message . . .

There was a flash from the speedboat and one of the wheelhouse ports starred: the sharp crack of the explosion reached him. It was he who needed to get the message. They'd no intention of letting him sail as far downstream as the sea . . .

He altered course to starboard, to widen the gap between them. There was a second shot, but as far as he could tell the trawler yacht was not hit. Shooting accurately from the speedboat, even at this reduced speed, would be extremely difficult and that first shot had been a very lucky one.

There was a blast of sound, deeper and louder than before, from his other quarter. A shotgun, he judged, probably loaded with LG or SG, far more lethal at close quarters than any revolver or automatic since each cartridge contained eight or twelve pellets and these formed a rough pattern which meant that an exact aim was not so essential.

He altered course to port, then back to starboard. The speedboats were more manoeuvrable and they had little difficulty in keeping clear. His last turn had brought him too far over to starboard and he'd passed outside the line of buoys, putting him in some danger—though with the tide still high, perhaps not too much—of running aground. As he put on port helm, he saw abeam a thin gleam of water: the mouth of one of the myriad creeks which criss-crossed the mudflats. It occurred to him that there was a maze which might just confuse pursuers . . .

Both speedboats dropped back and for a moment he thought they'd given up. But ahead were the steaming lights of an oncoming boat under power and he realized they'd fallen back in order not to arouse any suspicions in the minds of those aboard the oncoming boat. So did he make some sort of distress signal? But if the oncoming craft stopped to find out what was the trouble, those aboard would be murdered because the men who were trying to kill him wouldn't hesitate to kill others to protect themselves . . . . He reduced revs until he'd no more than steering way as the current carried him downstream. He again checked aft. Now, it was very difficult to make out the speedboats. The men aboard them would be waiting for him to make a move, confident that whatever it turned out to be they could counter it. But had they realized how desperate a desperate man could become? He looked round the wheelhouse. The craft was well found and maintained and somewhere there would be an emergency hand pump, ready to take over if the mechanical pumps failed. There were three lockers for'd. Briefly leaving the wheel each time, he checked the lockers: none of them contained a pump. So where would it be stored? Somewhere handy because if it was wanted, it would be wanted in a hurry. He remembered the locker by the ladder leading down to the after deck. He steered well out into the channel because tide and single screws were, if unchecked, bringing her head round, then left the wheel and hurried out of the wheelhouse.

The large metal locker was to port of the ladder. There were provisions for a padlock—to be used in port—but none was fitted and the lid was secured only by clamps. As he released the first of these, he heard from ahead the single blast of a foghorn. The helmsman on the oncoming boat was reminding him to keep to his side of the channel: tide and single screw were having more effect than he'd judged . . . He released the last clamp and threw open the lid which crashed back against the rails. The inside of the locker was too dark for him to make out what was there, but when he put his hands inside he felt something that had to be a pump. As he brought it out, a box fell and spilled its contents and some of these rolled against his right hand. Keeping hold of the pump in his left hand—and careless how the rubber hose coiled itself into confusion—he reached back into the locker and brought out three of the tubular objects. They were flares.

He raced back up the ladder and into the wheelhouse. The oncoming craft sounded its hooter twice to show it was making an emergency turn to port, the only way in which a collision could now be avoided. Sterne steered further to port and the two craft passed each other with less than six feet between them. From the other craft there came a blasphemous commentary on Sterne's navigational abilities, his seamanship, and his ancestry.

The two speedboats had fallen back and were no longer visible to him although it was likely that he was still visible to them since he was outlined by the newly risen moon. It was now or never. He increased revs and steered into the mouth of one of the creeks.

When he'd been young, there'd been a machine in the penny arcades in which a model car was suspended above a road imprinted on a drum which revolved: such had been the speed of the drum that there'd been no chance of correctly following the road and the car had pursued a crazy path across pavements and through houses . . . He rounded the first bend and reduced speed. Ahead, the channel divided into three, each channel slightly narrower than the one he was in. It was a complete lottery so he steered for the right-hand one. Almost immediately, that divided into two. He again chose the right-hand one. The mud banks closed until it seemed they must entrap him, but then they drew apart again and the keel remained free . . . Another division and this time he chose to go left. They'd be able to see his mast and superstructure above the mudflats, but since the channels twisted and turned to the point where it was impossible to know in which direction they were really heading, that wouldn't tell them immediately which way to steer.

He reduced speed still further until he was doing no more than breasting the ebbing water. Now, the bows would almost certainly swing one way or the other and ground, but grounding couldn't affect the success or failure of what he was going to do. He left the wheelhouse and began to search the decks, looking for a fuel tank filler cap. He found the starboard one as the trawler yacht shuddered slightly as she went aground. The cap had a bar centre, but when he tried to turn this, the cap remained fast. He cursed as he used the heel of his shoe to kick it and either the curse or the blow worked because the cap eased free and he was able to unscrew it. He fed the hose down the lead and just before he came to the end of this he felt it meet the bottom of the tank. He began to pump. For a while nothing happened, then the pumping became harder and he heard the irregular sounds of liquid splashing into the water. He smelled the coarse, pungent stench of diesel oil.

In the moonlight, by now quite strong, he could see the

rainbow sheen of the oil spreading and drifting with the water. He heard the powerboats' engines come close, then they became more distant. If they'd made a wrong turn, they'd soon realize it when his mast drew too far away for the cause to be solely the twists of the channel. With their manœuvrability, it wouldn't be difficult to retrace their course and find the right channel. And they wouldn't be worried. If he stayed on the yacht, they'd soon have him, if he took to the mudflats, those would soon have him—every year, wildfowlers were drowned when they were only a short way out from land and now he was over half a mile away. He increased the rate of pumping.

The sound of the engines came closer and this time did not fade. Holding the pump with his knees, he used his free hand to bring out one of the flares from his pocket. It was six inches long, an inch and a half in diameter, brown in colour, and the cap and tab were silver.

The nearest bend was a hundred yards away. The first powerboat slowly rounded it. Someone aboard shouted; there was an echoing call from the second boat.

He stopped pumping and pulled off the tab of the flare. Flame and thick orange smoke spurted out. Keeping the flare in his left hand, he played the flame on the oily water while resuming pumping with his right hand. The smoke, drifting with the wind, was forming billows and these rolled towards the powerboats, dropping a curtain between him and them. There were shouts of anger and guns were fired: a couple of yards out from the hull, the water suddenly erupted as several pellets hit it.

The powerboats came forward, feeling their way through the smoke. Someone called to go more quickly and get in and kill the bastard: someone else said they couldn't go any quicker in the smoke. The flare came to an end. The smoke rolled over the powerboats, leaving visibility in its wake. As Sterne pulled the other two flares out of his pocket, the nearer powerboat closed. For a couple of seconds he pumped as quickly as he could, then he dropped the pump, pulled the tags off the flares, and directed the flames on to the oily surface. He moved aft, keeping pace with the flow of water so that the flames played on the same area and heated the oil to higher and higher temperatures. An automatic cracked twice, then the shotgun boomed. His shoulder felt as if it had been kicked by a mule and he fell back, dropping the flares. He must have been visible through the smoke because there was a shout of triumph . . .

The oil ignited. A wall of flame spread out and raced forward. It reached and engulfed the two powerboats before the occupants had really understood what was happening. They screamed as the flames surrounded and beat down on them and instinctively they tried to jump into the flaming water, desperate to quench the burning agony. But there was one explosion, quickly followed by another, which sent shock waves rolling. The screaming ceased. And when the last of the debris had fallen back the only sounds were those of the water, chuckling as it made its way towards the main channel and the sea.

CHAPTER 23

Afterwards, for Sterne the night was a series of hazy, unchronological memories. There was the horrible sickness of knowing that he'd killed the four men and it made no difference knowing that if he hadn't killed them, they'd have killed him; the effort it cost him to bypass the port engine switch and start that engine; the impotent, childish anger when she refused to pull free even with both engines going full astern; the pain; the snatches of wild conversation that seemed to come from beyond the boat; the way the boat heeled as the waterlevel dropped; the shooting star which was supposed to foretell good luck, not disaster . . .

With daylight, he regained a degree of comprehension and judgement, and when the rising tide was almost at the full, he started the engines once more and went astern. Reluctantly, the boat slowly pulled free of the mud.

There was just room to swing her and he succeeded in doing this at the cost of twice running aground—each time she pulled free. He chose the correct route back to the buoyed channel even though he had not consciously made a note of the way he'd taken. In the buoyed channel, he headed upstream. He did not collapse until alongside the outboard jetty of the marina.

The late afternoon was hot and sunny as Sterne sat out in the hospital's grounds, his arm in a sling. He did not hear or see Young approach and was startled by the words: ' 'Afternoon, so how's the shoulder?'

He turned. Young, and a second man, stood a couple of feet away. 'It feels as if it's been through the mincer, but supposedly it's getting better.'

'That's good. You were lucky.'

'We must have a different definition of "lucky".'

'The last man I saw who'd been shot with buckshot was on the mortuary slab.' There was a wrought-iron garden chair nearby and Young moved this close to the wooden chair on which Sterne sat. He indicated his companion. 'I think you've already met Detective-Constable Icks of the local force?'

Sterne nodded.

'I came along to tell you how things are. I was called up from Kent to see if I could help and after I read your statements I suggested someone had a much closer look at *Morag III*.'

'We'd have got round to that on our own account,' said Icks grittily.

'Perhaps,' replied Young, showing no desire to be tactful. 'They'd searched her and told me she was clean. I said to look again because no one was going to sell me the coincidence that she was down in Cala Survas by chance.'

'We'd have looked again,' said Icks.

This time, Young ignored him. 'They finally found the locker in the bilges, hidden behind a false wall—or whatever that's called in a boat. It was empty, but there were enough traces to prove that it had carried heroin—not that the traces have yet been definitively analysed, but there's no doubt.'

'She was running drugs?'

'Dead right.' Young turned to Icks. It's a lovely day for a walk, Jim.'

'My guv'nor told me to stay . . .'

'It's quite all right. Mr Sterne and I have finished with the business and now we've a private matter to discuss.'

Icks would have liked to call Young a liar, but his respect for rank, even when not of his own force, was too great. He walked away.

'A good lad, but a sight too serious,' said Young. 'I don't think you've really appreciated the significant point of what I've just told you.'

'Isn't it the obvious one? The boat was carrying drugs.'

'There's more to it than that.'

Sterne was surprised how the underlying suggestion of antagonism which there had once been in Young's manner was now gone.

'Tell me what happened on your second visit to Lençon,' continued Young.

'I've only been there the once.'

'Twice. The second time just before the crash.'

'I wasn't in that car crash . . .'

'Let me explain something. When the case suddenly

became far more serious, I felt entitled to get on to the French police, not to prove that you'd been over there on your brother's passport, but to discover what had happened in the crash. They told me it had been a damned funny one and they'd been unable to come to any firm decision about it. Ralph Sterne's car had been forced off the road and it seemed certain the other driver had either been trying to kill him or had been drunk. But the lorry-driver testified that after the crash the Peugeot was being driven as steady as a rock . . . They were trying to kill you, weren't they?'

It was ridiculous, Sterne thought, to go on denying the obvious fact that he'd been in France. 'Yes.'

'Why?'

'God knows.'

'There has to be a reason. Think. Did you recognize someone at the motel?'

'No.'

'What happened there and who did you speak to?'

Sterne told him how they'd questioned the manager and the chambermaid and then returned the following morning to question the manager a second time.

'What did he tell you that was so dangerous for you to know?'

'He didn't tell me anything of any consequence.'

'And the chambermaid?'

'No help either.'

'Goddamn it, there must have been something. You didn't talk to anyone else?'

'Only the night handyman who'd been given the sack for being a Peeping Tom.'

'Tell me about him.'

'There's nothing to tell. He used a periscope to see hotel guests having fun and games. I asked him about the night of the twelfth and whether he'd looked in on cabin fifty-two and the Bressonauds. He had, but had not seen anything of interest.'

'Did he detail what he did see?'

'Madame Bressonaud in bed. The sight wasn't one to excite even him, so he moved on.'

'What about the husband?'

'He wasn't around and her clothes were on the second bed. As a matter of fact, I got to wondering if he'd ever actually turned up. After all, you don't put clothes on a bed that's going to be used. Funny thing is, though, the chambermaid said both beds had been slept in.'

'Did you ask who'd booked in?'

'The wife, for the two of them. The receptionist supposedly remembers seeing him, but I don't think he really did.'

'Well I'll be damned!' Young puffed his cheeks. 'Well, I'll be doubly damned!'

'All right, you're thoroughly damned. Why?'

'Because I'd forgotten how the obvious can become obscure. And the way in which the guilty give themselves away because they invariably believe the innocent think, as they do, in a guilty manner . . . They tried to kill you in the car in France because you'd discovered there was no husband at the motel. It never occurred to them that you wouldn't, couldn't, see the significance of that fact.'

'They were right; I didn't, I couldn't, I still can't.'

'Right at the beginning, the point your brother made about the police watch at the Newingreen motel worried me. So when we finally found the container on *Morag III*, I got to wondering about some other points; why the mob should have bothered to try as well to smuggle a very much smaller quantity of heroin in by car, driven by an innocent; and why the informer, who had to be very close to the centre if he knew not only that a load was hidden in the car you were driving but also what cross-Channel boat you'd be on, hadn't known about this much larger consignment and grassed on that as well?'

'I don't understand what you're getting at.'

'The container in the Mercedes could hold between a third and half a million pounds' worth of heroin. When that sort of money's at stake, every possible precaution's taken to make certain nothing goes wrong and in particular that no one is ever in a position where he or she can take off and disappear with the consignment. So if the container had contained heroin, Mr Bressonaud would have been around to keep an eye on Mrs Bressonaud, just as Mrs Bressonaud would have kept an eye on Mr Bressonaud—and I hope I don't have to add that they would not, in fact, have been man and wife. That there was only the woman must mean there was no fortune in heroin.'

Sterne stared at him. 'You're saying . . . that the container in the Mercedes didn't contain heroin?'

'Only sufficient traces to make us believe it must have been full.'

'But why?'

'To make us assume—as we did—that a fresh line had been started, using cars from the south of France, so that we'd keep the closest possible watch on that route. And what was the point of that? It's hard fact that if you have limited manpower and need to concentrate on one particular aspect of your work, other aspects must inevitably suffer. So in this case they were making certain that a boat arriving from Spain would probably not be subjected to more than a cursory search. In other words, you were sucker-bait.'

'I didn't smuggle in heroin, either knowingly or unknowingly?'

'Technically, I can't answer as to the smuggling—I don't know whether the traces found constitute a sufficient quantity to fall within the legal definition of smuggling. That you didn't know what was going on, I now have not the slightest doubt.'

'Then what happens about my case?'

'Proceedings were adjourned because of your injury. All fresh evidence will be sent to the DPP who'll undoubtedly order that at the trial no evidence is submitted by the prosecution and, I imagine, that a statement is made making it quite clear that you were innocent of knowingly trying to import drugs.'

Sterne found it difficult fully to comprehend that his nightmare was over.

'You will still be faced with two proceedings. There'll be an inquiry into the deaths of the men who were trying to kill you—even if it's clear that you were justified in what you did—and you'll be charged with attempting to import a vehicle without paying the appropriate tax.'

'To hell with that!'

'I imagine most people will echo those sentiments.'

Sterne said: 'I can return to France?'

'As soon as I've arranged for the handing back of your passport. I think it'll be best for everyone if you travel on yours next time.' He stood.

'I owe you a lot.'

'Do you? It's probably more accurate to say that really you've got yourself to thank—a case of justice unjustly served but justly found . . . But if you should feel slightly in debt . . .' He stopped.

'Yes?'

'You might tell me how in the hell you got back into this country. I've been losing sleep trying to work it out.'

'That's an official secret.'

Young murmured gloomily: 'I thought you'd say something like that.' He failed to realize his question had been answered.

Sterne drove up to L'Ile Blanche and parked in front of the bronze door. De Matour came out of the house and embraced him with Gallic lack of restraint while the two borzois appeared and barked with enthusiasm. 'Belinda's gone with Evelyn into Chinon to do some shopping, but they should be back soon . . . And how have things been with you?'

'It's a long story, but basically I'm a free man.'

'Then we shall open a bottle of champagne to celebrate.' He put his arm round Sterne's shoulders in a gesture of affection. He felt Sterne flinch. 'What is this?'

'I was shot in the shoulder, but I'm virtually OK now.'

'When a man is shot he needs two bottles of champagne, not one.'

They went inside. They had not quite finished the first bottle when a car drew up outside the front door. 'Stay here,' said de Matour. 'I will send her in.'

Sterne heard Evelyn ask her husband: 'Whose car is that, Jean?'

'A visitor's.'

'Of course it's a visitor's. You really can be very annoying. Is it someone for whom I need go upstairs and make myself attractive?'

'You are attractive now, without going anywhere.'

'Something's happened. You're talking stupidly and you look like a Cheshire cat?'

'What is special about a Cheshire cat?'

'You pride yourself on being literate and you've never read Lewis Carroll? . . . For goodness sake, who is our caller?'

'He says his name is Angus.'

Sterne heard the sound of running feet and then the door was flung open and Belinda rushed into the room.

Other Titles in the Walker British Mystery Series

MARIAN BABSON • Bejewelled Death
Dangerous to Know
Death Warmed Up
Line Up for Murder

JOHN CREASEY • The Baron in France
The Baron on Board
Help from the Baron
Hide the Baron
Last Laugh for the Baron
The Toff and the Fallen Angels
Trap the Baron

ELIZABETH LEMARCHAND • Change for the Worse
Cyanide with Compliments
Nothing to Do with the Case
No Vacation from Murder
Step in the Dark
Suddenly While Gardening
Troubled Waters
Unhappy Returns
The Wheel Turns

BEN HEALEY • Midnight Ferry to Venice

KENNETH GILES • Death Among the Stars
Death and Mr. Prettyman
Death Cracks a Bottle
A File on Death
Murder Pluperfect
Some Beasts No More

ANGUS ROSS • Ampurias Exchange
The Burgos Contract
Hamburg Switch

W.J. BURLEY • Charles and Elizabeth
Death in a Salubrious Place
Death in Stanley Street
Death in Willow Pattern
The House of Care
The Schoolmaster
To Kill a Cat
Wycliffe and the Schoolgirls